# Second Chance with My Bull Rider

Cowboys of Sunnydale, Volume 2

Allie Bock

Published by Allie Bock, 2020.

# Table of Contents

Copyright Page .................................................................................. 1
Dedication ........................................................................................ 2
Acknowledgments ........................................................................... 3
More Books by Allie Bock ............................................................... 4
Newsletter ........................................................................................ 5
Chapter 1 August 2nd ..................................................................... 6
Chapter 2 August 2nd ................................................................... 13
Chapter 3 August 9th .................................................................... 23
Chapter 4 August 11th .................................................................. 31
Chapter 5 August 15th .................................................................. 35
Chapter 6 September 1st ............................................................... 56
Chapter 7 September 1st ............................................................... 65
Chapter 8 September 1st ............................................................... 71
Chapter 9 September 8th .............................................................. 81
Chapter 10 September 9th ............................................................ 94
Chapter 11 October 3rd .............................................................. 105
Chapter 12 October 4th .............................................................. 116
Chapter 13 October 4th .............................................................. 120
Chapter 14 October 10th ............................................................ 131
Chapter 15 October 10th ............................................................ 137
Chapter 16 October 17th ............................................................ 142
Chapter 17 October 23rd ............................................................ 148
Chapter 18 October 23rd ............................................................ 153
Chapter 19 November 9th .......................................................... 156
Chapter 20 November 9th Later That Afternoon ................... 163
Chapter 21 November 9th .......................................................... 171
Chapter 22 November 14th ........................................................ 181
Chapter 23 December 20th ........................................................ 184
Epilogue January ......................................................................... 190

Newsletter .................................................................................. 193

# Copyright Page

*Copyright © 2020 by Allie Bock*
*All rights reserved. No part of this publication may be reproduced, stored, or transmitted in any form or by any means, electronic, mechanical, photocopying, recording, scanning, or otherwise without written permission from the publisher. It is illegal to copy this book, post it to a website, or distribute it by any other means without permission.*

*This novel is entirely a work of fiction. The names, characters, and incidents portrayed in it are the work of the author's imagination. Any resemblance to actual persons, living or dead, events or localities is entirely coincidental.*

*Cover Design by Tugboat Design*

*First edition*

# Dedication

*Jill and Nathan for being the best parents a girl could ask for. Thank you for believing in my dreams.*

# Acknowledgments

*Writing a book takes a lot of time and effort, and I couldn't do it by myself. First off, thank you to Derek and Zack for reading and editing my story. Thank you to all the wonderful beta readers for giving me valuable feedback.*

# More Books by Allie Bock

Cowboys of Sunnydale Series:[1]
My Cowboy Crush[2]
Falling for My Cowboy[3]
Second Chance with My Bull Rider[4]

---

1. https://www.alliebock.com/p/allies-books.html
2. https://www.alliebock.com/p/my-cowboy-crush.html
3. https://www.alliebock.com/p/falling-for-my-cowboy.html
4. https://www.alliebock.com/p/second-chance-with-my-bull-rider.html

# Newsletter

If you like what you are reading and want to keep in touch sign up for my NEWSLETTER[1]. You will receive an Alternative Ending for joining the newsletter.

---

1. htttps://www.subscribepage.com/secondchancewithmybullrideraltend

# Chapter 1 August 2nd

## Delilah

The sun streamed into the indoor arena of the Happy Hearts Therapeutic Riding Center, falling on the butterflies and sunflowers painted in bright colors on the walls. Dust motes danced in the sunlight. The laughter of children filled the air along with the methodical thud of hooves and the gentle snorts from the horses.

I sighed. I loved being here, volunteering with the children, and working with horses. I needed to get out of the emergency room in San Antonio. Being an emergency room nurse had been my dream, but now it sucked the life out of me. I dreaded going to work and I no longer felt the spike of adrenaline when helping patients. On my days off, I desired to be at a place where happiness and laughter were the norm, like here.

A lock of hair fell forward into my eyes. I tucked it behind my ear, pulling my baseball cap down further on my head. I turned to the child, Tabitha, riding the pony I led. A smile adorned her face, splitting it from ear to ear. Her eyes sparkled with delight while the pony took small, slow steps forward. Two other volunteers walked alongside Tabitha with their hands on her rail-thin thighs. I caught their grins when Tabitha set a rubber ball in the matching bucket. One volunteer high-fived her while I steered the little chestnut pony onto the next obstacle. We followed the bay horse, Jasper, ahead of us, making our way around the little course. We walked over a bridge, dropped a small rubber hoop on a cone, and picked up a toy from one bucket to carry it to the next bucket. Some of the obstacles were more difficult than others for Tabitha, but she finished the course with a wide smile.

"You did wonderful today, Tabitha!" I said when we stopped next to her mother and a miniature wheelchair. I was proud of her as if she was my child.

"I did everything by myself!" She crowed. Her pigtails bounced on her shoulders. The copper pony looked back at her. "And Penny was great."

"Just like always." I rubbed the little pony on the forehead.

Leah, lead instructor, owner, and organizer of the Happy Hearts Therapeutic Riding Center, walked to the center of the sand arena and raised her hands in the air. She cleared her voice before addressing the students, parents, and volunteers, all twenty-five people present. "Great lesson everyone! You probably don't need to be reminded, but next week we are going to have our end of the session show, so make sure to bring a dish to pass and all your smiling faces."

A cheer went up from the children.

"Also," she continued, "as we discussed a couple of weeks ago, next week is the last week Happy Hearts will be in operation. You can bring lots of carrots and apples for your ponies. They will be joining our party, too."

The cheers quieted as soon as the words left her lips, popping the happiness like a bubble, leaving only sadness and stillness behind. With subdued tones, we assisted the children off their ponies and horses and into their wheelchairs. Tabitha reached into the pocket attached to the side of her wheelchair, extracting a horse treat. She extended her little hand toward the pony's soft nose. Penny nuzzled her hand, gently taking the treat. Her whiskers tickled Tabitha's palm and she giggled.

I patted the pony's neck as bittersweet nostalgia filled my chest. The children enjoyed every moment spent with the horses and this was my escape from my reality. It reminded me of the good parts of my childhood and teen years, spending time riding with friends out in open spaces, laughing, and enjoying time in the sun. Now, I spend my days in the glass and concrete emergency room, listening to the beeping of monitors, and hurried calls of the orderlies. It was a long way from my country roots.

I led the pony into her stall. I pulled off her saddle and bridle and brushed her. Leah slowly walked down the aisle after the children left, checking on all the horses and volunteers, and making small talk with each person until she reached the stall I was in with Penny at the end of the barn.

"Tabitha is coming along nicely," she said. She held out a peppermint to the pony.

"She is." I lifted one hoof to clean out the sand and pebbles. "It's none of my business to ask, but why are you closing the stable." I straightened to watch the expressions flit across her face, from sadness to a contained excitement.

"The army is transferring my husband out east in the next couple of months. I didn't want to start another session just to end it early." She fed Penny another peppermint. Her eyes were sad when they met mine. "I'll miss the children."

"I know you will." I reached out my hand to rest it on her arm. "Isn't it closer to your family?"

"Yes, I haven't seen them in years, and no one is getting younger."

I laughed at that. "None of us are." I slipped the halter over Penny's ears to release her. "What's going to happen to this place?"

"I don't know. If someone can take over the lease, the owners might let it keep operating. I have two months until I leave to figure it out." Her eyes cut to me, with a gleam in them that I knew was never good. "How about you take it over?"

"Me?" I dropped the grooming bucket, scattering brushes everywhere.

"Yes, of course!" She clapped her hands with excitement, causing Penny to snort at her. "You've been around horses your whole life and you're great with the kids."

"But I have a full-time job at the hospital."

"Think about it," she shrugged before walking down the barn aisle.

"She's crazy," I rubbed Penny between the eyes as she nudged my pockets for treats.

THE MONITORS BEEPED in another room. People scurried around, calling to each other. I sat at the nurses' station trying to fill out paperwork for the last patient I'd seen. I stared at the computer screen for what seemed like the hundredth time.

"Hey, Delilah, are you almost done?" Chad, my supervisor, asked. "You've been at it for a while."

"I can't seem to focus today."

"I've noticed." He laid a hand on my shoulder. "Is everything O.K.?"

A moment or two passed before I could respond. *How do I tell him how I feel? What would he say?* "Yes, everything is fine."

"You haven't been yourself for the last couple of weeks." He set his clipboard down and leaned against the counter. "You're coming in later than normal, leaving at lunchtime, and just overall distracted. The doctors have been making comments to me on your mental health, especially Dr. Glanders."

I sighed and tried not to roll my eyes. Of course, Dr. Greg Glanders would be worried about me. We dated for a bit, but I broke it off after a couple of weeks. He was a great guy, just boring. We parted as friends, at least on my side. I knew he wanted to be more than that. I missed the excitement and the zing that I had with my first and only love. Instead, I said, "I've had a lot on my mind."

What I wanted to tell him was that I had grown to resent my job, waking up in time for work was difficult, and all I wanted to do was go to bed when I got home. Not to mention, my mind wandered over to Happy Hearts Therapeutic Riding Center and thought about everything I could do there: the children I could help, horses to be cared for, the barn needed to be painted, the fences mended, and whatever else Leah needed. The stable was the bright spot in my week.

"You're getting burnt out," he said softly, breaking into my thoughts. "You've been here for six years without a vacation. No one can work the hours you've been keeping...I want you to go home early, your shift is almost over anyway. And tomorrow I want you to come in and let me know how long you're going to be gone on vacation and where you're going."

"Seriously?" My eyebrows raised in surprise.

"Kid, you need a break. Not to mention, you are a liability if you start messing things up with patients."

I cringed at his words. He was right.

"We can handle everything while you take a couple of weeks off. The ER will be fine if Delilah Allen takes a vacation. We'll be here when you get back." He clapped me on the back, grabbed his clipboard, and hurried off down the hall.

"What am I going to do with a vacation?" I said to myself as I grabbed my things.

On the way back to my apartment, I made a detour to the library which sat close to downtown San Antonio. I parked my car in the parking ramp and walked a couple of blocks to the library. It was a beautiful day for South Texas in August. It was hot but a stiff breeze made it comfortable to be outside. The library doors loomed ahead of me and slid open silently as I approached. The cold air inside caused goosebumps to race up my arms. I shivered, hugging my arms to my chest.

"May I help you, ma'am?" The woman at the desk asked.

"Um," I glanced around. It was huge, much bigger than the library in my hometown of Sunnydale that was thirty miles away. There was even an elevator with a list of floors next to it. I turned back to her, a little overwhelmed. "I think I just need a computer."

"Absolutely, I'll need your driver's license or another form of identification." She handed me a sheet of paper covered in small print. "These are the instructions on how to log onto the internet."

I exchanged my license for the paper as she tapped away on the keyboard before giving my license back and pointing me on my way.

The computer lab was cool and quiet, filled with little clicks as people typed away on the keys. I weaved my way to computer number 32 and set my bag down. Following the instructions on the sheet of paper, I logged in and searched for any information on therapeutic riding centers in Texas.

After a few hours, my eyes were sore, my back hurt, and the tips of my fingers were numb, but I held in my hand several sheets on how to become certified to run a therapeutic riding center. My body was physically tired from work and concentrating on the computer, yet my heart was excited with the new prospects on the horizon. Chad was right, I was feeling burnt out from my job as a nurse, which I had been doing since college.

Sometimes, I needed to work to distract me from the memories that crept up on me at home. The love and family that I almost had but lost, the pain and the loneliness that filled every corner of my small apartment, and the longing for a child that I may never have. Shaking my head to clear my thoughts, I folded the paper and placed it in my bag to head home. Maybe, just maybe, I could do something different. I'd still be helping people. I'd be making a difference in the lives of others. With a conviction I hadn't felt in a long time, I decided on what I'd be telling Chad in the morning: that I needed a permanent break from the hospital.

# Chapter 2 August 2nd

## Kade

The bull snorted underneath me, as he shifted his weight from side to side, swinging his horns at the gate. A jarring shot threw me as I tightened down my bull rope; luckily, a hand grabbed the back of my vest to keep me centered. Settling on the bull's back, I took a moment. The crowd cheered. He snorted and pawed the ground. Sweat dripped from my brow. I nodded to open the gate. The latch clicked and the door flung open with a screech. The bull burst through the gate, leaving the ground behind us. One jump, two jump, and a spin. My muscles flexed and strained as I stayed at the center of his back. We were like a pair of dancers at a dance-off. I met him move for move. The dirt flew and the pounding of hooves filled my ears. I almost had him, only a few more seconds to go. In a surge of power, the bull jumped into the air, rolling his back like an alligator. My feet slipped back as my hand popped out of the rope. The earth quickly met me, filling my mouth with its sandy texture. A silence fell over the crowd.

A loud repetitive beeping startled me awake, taking the place of the rhythm of the pounding hooves. Something pinched the crook of my elbow and my back was stiff from laying on a hard mattress. My eyelids cracked open a bit, and I rolled to my side to look around. Hard plastic chairs stood empty against the back wall. Next to me was a machine and an IV line, pumping a clear liquid into my veins. Slowly, I directed my gaze over to the other side. A bed with crisp white sheets stood unoccupied beside mine. A couple of stuffed chairs were sitting between the two beds. Someone unfolded themselves and approached me.

"Well, look who is back in the land of the living." A familiar deep voice rumbled. I knew only one person with that voice: my big brother, Kaleb. I groaned. I must have been in bad shape for him to leave the ranch. He never left the ranch.

"Where am I?" My throat was scratchy, and my lips cracked.

"East Texas Hospital," he said. He pushed the chair he was napping in closer to my side. The scraping of wood on the tile worsened the ache at my temple. I closed my eyes again. *How did I end up here?* As much as I tried, I couldn't remember. The pain blocked out everything that had happened. Was it earlier today, two days ago, or several weeks? A groan escaped me as I rolled over to my side. The IV pulled at my arm, the pounding grew in my head, and lightning bolts of pain shot around my chest.

"I see Mr. Kisment's awake." A nurse pulled a cart through the door, the wheels screeching in protest as light flooded the room from the hallway. "Now's a good time for all your pain medications." She adjusted some pillows behind me on the bed and injected several substances into the port of my IV. "There, you'll feel better in no time." She hurried out of the room.

"What happened to me?" I growled towards my brother, frustrated at the lack of answers. His deep laugh answered sarcastically from somewhere in the shadows.

"You pulled a bull no one rode in a long time," He paused. "You got a little beat up on the dismount."

"A little beat up? I feel like a train ran over me."

"Nope, just at two-thousand-pound animal ground you into the dirt." His voice was quieter than before.

"How long have I been here?" I pinched the bridge of my nose with my free hand.

"Only two days."

His words stunned me. I had been unconscious for two days! How bad were my injuries? "How many?"

"How many what?" He asked.

*Was he trying to be dense?* "Injuries," I said

"The doc said you are lucky to be alive."

"What does that mean?" I growled, quickly losing my patience

"A concussion, several broken ribs, a broken tibia and fibula, and your ankle is crushed. The doc said that you tore all the ligaments in your ankle." He ticked off on his fingers like he had repeated it several times.

My heart pounded in my chest as the room went eerily quiet. I had been injured before. Earlier this summer, I sustained a concussion when in San Antonio, but that was child's play compared to this. The pain radiated up my side with every breath I took causing my eyes to water.

"Alright." I gritted out. "How long?"

"How long for what?"

"How long until I can ride again?"

He got up from the chair and moved to stare down at me. His eyebrows hooded his dark blue eyes. An unreadable expression crossed his face. He swiped a hand through his light brown hair. "Best case, six months."

Math was never my strong suit. Quickly, I counted the months, which was hard considering the concussion. That would put me into next year, and I would miss the Bull Riding Finals. There went the buckle I desperately wanted to win. There went all my hard work the last eleven years and the dream that I worked so hard to get.

"That's not acceptable." I slurred some swear words as the pain medication caused the room to go fuzzy, and then black as I drifted off to a night of drug-induced sleep.

An incessant beeping disturbed me from my sleep. The shuffle of feet and frenzied voices slipped through the crack in the door. The light from the main room crept into my room about two feet. It illuminated Kaleb's form, slouched over in the armchair. I stared at the blank ceiling. Six months was a long time, and this year was going to be the year I won big as it was finally going my way, but my dreams for the championship were squashed worse than I was. The disappointment and heartache overwhelmed the physical pain in my body. I reached for the IV in my arm and with one pull I yanked it out. Blood gushed over the sheets. I grabbed the tissues and packed them into the crook of my elbow. Next, the monitors came off. A blaring noise erupted from the machines. I gingerly sat up and panted as I gathered myself.

"What do you think you are doing?" Kaleb glowered down at me. We were both about the same size, but whereas I kept down to a lean weight, he bulked up from doing hard physical labor every day on the ranch. In the dark, he was a menacing figure to cross.

"I am going home," I crossed my arms.

Muttering some curses, he said, "no you're not. Not until the doctor releases you." He shoved me back onto the bed and held me down until a nurse burst through the door. She assessed the situation before breaking into action and calling for back up.

"I'm going home." I glared at the nurses as blood dripped down my arm, hitting the floor. "I can sleep better there." I took a chance and jutted out my chin like a child, but the night nurses were a mean group, and it didn't faze them. A nurse grabbed each of my arms and held me in the bed. Their hands put pressure on my shoulders, pushing me deeper into the hard mattress. An older nurse came in and started to reattach the monitors. She applied a bandage to my bleeding arm.

"Take these." She thrust a small white cup with several pills into my good hand. "The doctor will talk to you in the morning. If you don't take it, we will sedate you and put the IV back in." Her black eyes drilled holes into me, daring me to refuse her. I was outnumbered and outmaneuvered, for now. With a sigh, I settled into the pillows and swallowed the medications, glaring at Kaleb. I didn't want to be sedated. He stood back in the shadows with a smirk playing on his lips while the nurses reattached me to the monitors.

The next morning, a tall woman in a white lab coat swept into the room, startling Kaleb who yanked his cowboy hat from his head. She glided across the floor and handed a clipboard with several sheets of paper to him, gracing him with a wide smile. "Good morning, Mr. Kisment."

"Good morning ma'am...I mean Doctor Finney," Kaleb stuttered. He stared at the papers she had handed him.

"Those are Kade's discharges," her eyes twinkled at him.

He mumbled a thank you and looked at his cowboy boots. I tried to hold in my smirk. Kaleb always had women throwing themselves at him, and he never knew what to do with them. My mother said it was his heart of gold that attracted them. I snorted, breaking the moment for them.

"I see you're awake." She moved over to me and started to examine the bandages, listen to my lungs, and examine my eyes. She asked about my pain level, had me counting, saying my birthday, and listing off my address. "Well, Kade, you are stable this morning and the bloodwork from yesterday came back normal. You are set to go home if you follow these instructions. I have you scheduled in two days with an orthopedic surgeon in San Antonio to repair your leg." She handed me another clipboard to sign my name and I was free to go.

If I had to pick one word to describe the ride back home, it would be miserable. Kaleb dumped me into the passenger seat of my old Ford pickup, which wasn't a comfortable ride on a good day. The seat was worn out and covered with a horse blanket. Half of the seat was taken up by Zip, my blue heeler, who was a little older than the truck. The shocks and struts were lacking, and it rattled as it went down the road. Every jar sent a tremor of pain across my chest and down my leg where it was propped up on the dashboard into a stretch no man should be comfortable making. My head pounded with every bump in the road.

"You're green, man." Kaleb glanced over at me before fiddling with the knob on the radio. "You're sure you're up to the four-hour drive back home?"

"Anything to get out of the hospital." A shudder ran through me as we merged onto the freeway. The cold window eased some of the headache and nausea.

"Hospitals ain't all bad." His words were barely more than a whisper.

"I know, but every time I am in one, it reminds me of that day."

Kaleb nodded and stared straight ahead. I fought back the thoughts that were trying to break free: memories that had been suppressed for eleven years, memories that were too painful to visit, and memories that had changed my life. That day, eleven years ago. I got a call from my fiancé's mother to go to the hospital. My beautiful Delilah was there looking so small and frail and in so much pain. And I just walked out because I couldn't do anything. I couldn't stand her misery. Our to-be-born baby died, and I couldn't do anything about it. Bile rose in the back of my mouth as I thought about the coward I had been and the mistake I made by not being there for her. Instead, I ran. I tortured myself with life on the road, chasing buckles.

"With all the money you win, you could own a better truck." He chuckled like it was the best joke he had ever made. His fist pounded the steering wheel.

"I like this truck," I muttered against the glass. My first kiss was in this truck. We had gone out to a far pasture my senior year in high school. She was a year younger than me and only a junior. She looked so pretty in the moonlight and I was so nervous. I wrapped my hands around her and brought her close before touching my lips to hers. They were soft and tasted of strawberries that she had brought to share.

"I know, I know. It's the first truck you bought." Kaleb added air quotes around the words, taking his hands from the wheel as the truck listed to the right.

"I say that a lot?" I lifted an eyebrow at him as the dull ache in my head moved around to the front of my head.

"Sure, do." He hummed along with the radio. "I think it has something to do with someone we don't talk about." His tuneless humming and Zip's snores filled the cab. I popped a couple more painkillers and closed my eyes. I prayed for a quick trip home with no more talking or memories of the only girl I ever loved.

I was jarred awake as Kaleb navigated my truck down the gravel road to the Kisment family ranch, the large sign with the Rocking K swinging next to the turnoff, an arrow pointing up the road. The way was full of potholes and shoulders that dropped off. He weaved his way through them trying to avoid the worst ones as a cloud of red dust flew behind us. I squinted out the windshield into the late afternoon sun. The grass turned a dead brown color with the only green on the landscape being clusters of cacti growing larger than a horse. The thin oak trees twisted their branches out to the side, while red cows huddled beneath the branches, looking for a respite from the sun. The calves chased each other around, ignoring the heat.

"Have you gotten any rain?" I asked.

"Nope, even the tanks are starting to dry up." He dodged a large hole before straightening the wheel. "Luckily, we had a good spring to make hay, before everything burnt up." He weaved to the left. "The well is full, so I've been pumping water for the cattle."

The cattle appeared content, chewing their cuds or sleeping in the shade as they lazily swiped at the flies buzzing around them. In the next field, several horses galloped up to the fence when the truck came into view. The chestnuts, bays, blacks, and my spotted Appaloosa, Apache, loped alongside the truck as we drove up to the gate, where Kaleb stopped with my side inches away from the metal pipe. I rolled my window down and leaned my elbows over the edge. Apache pushed the rest of the herd away as he stuck his head through the window.

"Don't have any treats this time, old boy." I rubbed his forehead. His soft muzzle nuzzled my shoulder. "It might be a while before I can ride you." When no food was produced, he ran back to the herd, and they galloped back out of sight. "He's fat," I said to Kaleb.

"No one rides him." The response had a bite to it. I turned to him in surprise, but he ignored me, continuing the way to the house.

The Kisment ranch sat at the end of the road. The truck rumbled over the cattle guard into the circular drive before the house where Kaleb parked in Ma's spot next to the door. Everything looked the same as it did when I left eleven years ago, never to come back until today. The house was a sprawling tan adobe with a rust-colored roof. The archways had hanging baskets of red geraniums. On the plank wrap-around porch, a couple of wicker chairs and a swing sat. Next to my truck, Kaleb's truck was parked under the overhang. Except, the yard was quiet.

"Where's all of Ma's chickens?" I opened the door to peer out around the yard.

"She gave them all away before they left." He got out and walked to my side, reaching for the wheelchair in the bed. I growled at him before reaching for my crutches from behind the seat.

"I am not using a wheelchair." I placed the crutch feet on the ground and contemplated how to best get out of the truck. "Where did they go?" I glanced up at Kaleb's frowning face.

"They're on a mission trip to Africa, where they've been for over a year... Do you want help?"

"No, I got this." I braced the pads in my armpits and swung from the seat to the ground. A swift, piercing pain split my side as I tried to keep in a scream. The blackness played with the edges of my vision. It closed around me. Kaleb's hands reached for me, settling me into the wheelchair. The blackness receded. I took in the smug look on his face when I glared up at him.

"I said I got it," I said, seething on the inside with pain and frustration.

"Sure, you did." He pushed my wheelchair up a makeshift ramp into the house to my bedroom. My prison for the foreseeable future.

# Chapter 3 August 9th

## Delilah

I hurried into the barn at Happy Hearts Therapeutic Riding Stable, glancing at my watch. Forty-five minutes remained until the students showed up for their last ride of the session. Leah was in the arena setting up the obstacle course for them to complete to graduate from this session. The horse's heads hung over their stall doors as I jogged down the barn aisle to the last stall. Penny's little soft nose was barely visible over the stall door. She nickered at my approach.

"Hey, girlie." I slipped the halter over her little ears. "I'm going to make you beautiful today." Clipping the lead rope onto her halter, I led her into the wash stall to bathe her.

I was combing out her tail when boot heels clicked down the aisle to the wash stall.

"Hi Delilah, it's good to see you here early this morning," Leah said. She leaned against the wall, crossing her long legs and arms.

"Yep, I wanted to get her clean for Tabitha today." I rinsed off the last of the soap from the pony.

Leah's lips tugged up into a smile, but it didn't reach her eyes. "They'd love that." She grabbed a comb and started to untangle Penny's unruly mane. "Did you think about taking over the riding stables?"

I nodded. Nothing else had been on my mind all week. I was on vacation and spending all my free time in the library, thinking about the children, the horses, and the riding stable. Some soul searching with my best friend, Melanie Baker, convinced me that taking over the therapeutic riding stable was where my life was headed.

"Good. The property owners will be here, after the show today. You should meet them." Leah set the comb down and went to visit with another volunteer.

"Did you hear that, Penny?" I whispered in the pony's little ear as it twitched towards me. "Maybe this will be easier than I thought."

The crunch of tires and slamming of doors broke the relative peace of the morning, announcing the arrival of the children.

"Delilah! I brought apple slices for Penny!" A giant smile covered Tabitha's face. Sarah pushed the wheelchair to a stop in front of the stall door. Penny blew out a soft nicker, straining at her lead rope trying to reach her partner in crime.

"She's going to love those." I crouched in front of the chair. "I have a surprise for you too." I reached into my back pocket and pulled out a tube.

"What is it?" She asked in an awed tone.

"It's glitter paint for horses. I thought we could draw some designs on her for fun."

Her eyes lit up as we painted handprints, flowers, and small suns on her side. Then, Tabitha wheeled up and down the barn aisle sharing the paint with her friends. My heart felt full as giggles and smiles filled the barn from the children that barely laughed at all.

"That was very nice," Sarah said, taking pictures of all sides of the pony. "It hasn't sunk in that this might be her last ride."

"Yeah," I slipped the bridle over her ears. I didn't know if I should tell her or not, but Sarah and I had gotten to be friends in the last six months. "I'm hopefully going to be taking it over...But don't say anything to the kids until I know for sure."

Her eyes lit up as she placed a hand on my shoulder. "I hope it works out, and I think you'll do great."

Leah clapped her hands. "Y'all, it's time for the horse show!" A cheer went up as we trooped to the arena.

An hour and a half later, the show wrapped up with Tabitha as the last rider. She dropped an apple into a bucket of water with a flourish. Penny stood stock still with her ears pricked forward as water splashed upon her. Cheers went up from the rest of the students, waiting on the sidelines. Tabitha fist-pumped the air. A large smile broke across her face as Sarah snapped pictures with wild abandon.

"I did it!" She shouted before reaching down to pet the pony's neck. The volunteers on each side of her gave her a high five. I was so proud of the little girl, almost as if she were my own. When she first arrived at Happy Hearts, Tabitha was sulky, miserable; she didn't interact with anyone and slouched in her wheelchair. Sarah was at her wit's end trying to brighten her little girl's life. Now, she babbled like a high running creek and was bursting with energy. Her transformation was what kept bringing me back to volunteer. In the emergency room, the tensions were high, and things were stressful. But here in the barn, people were excited to be a part of other people's lives. I sighed with contentment while I stroked Penny's shiny neck under her mane.

"You sure did, sweetie," Leah said. She placed a string of beads around Tabitha's neck, looping it twice, the green beads clashing with Tabitha's purple shirt. "Excellent job...Hey kids, time for cake and ice cream! Volunteers will untack the ponies and bring them back in for their treats."

We helped the children dismount and settle back into their wheelchairs, braces, or with their parents. Then, we walked the horses and ponies back to their stalls. The program was smaller than a lot of other therapeutic riding programs. There were only ten horses that the children could ride. Penny, being a Welsh pony, was the smallest. The black Percheron cross, Billy, was the largest. He carried the heavier riders. More gray hairs sprinkled throughout his black coat every year, giving him a distinguished look. Once each horse was in their stalls, we briskly removed the saddles and bridles, gave them a quick brushing, and led them back into the arena.

Leah brought each of us a piece of cake and ice cream while we held our charges. Then, the children came around and gave each one a piece of apple or a carrot. At the end of the party, an older couple walked through the door as Tabitha was giving Penny one last hug. Tears streamed down her cheeks and she hiccupped into Penny's mane. Penny wrapped her short, chubby neck around the little girl's frail shoulders to rest her chin on the girl's back. A fracture worked its way through my heart, causing my eyes to mist as I watched the pair. Sarah sniffled behind me. Her camera clicked as she shot a couple of last pictures of the two of them. Finally, Tabitha untangled her arms from Penny's neck and wiped at her tears.

"Are you ready to go, sweetie?" Sarah asked, leaning down to Tabitha's level. Tabitha nodded and turned to me.

"Are you going to take care of her?" Her little girl's voice squeaked.

"Yes, I will," I promised. I didn't know the logistics yet of how I would do that, but I would. She stuck up her little pinkie and

I wrapped mine around hers. "Pinkie swear," I whispered to her before Sarah pushed her out to the parking lot.

"Delilah, there is someone I want to introduce you to," Leah said. She led the older couple over to me. The woman picked her feet up high and carefully set them down, trying not to get dust or horse manure on her Italian flats. Her bejeweled fingers spread out to the side to help her balance and her husband held her other hand. His suit was crisp and clean. Obviously, they didn't spend time in the stables.

"Mr. and Mrs. Peterson, this is Delilah Allen. She's the one I was telling you about, how she'd like to take over my lease on the stable and continue Happy Hearts Therapeutic Riding Center."

"Oh yes, it's a pleasure to meet you, dear," Mrs. Peterson drawled as she held out a limp hand for me to shake. "Bless your heart for wanting to continue what our dear Leah started. We're sure going to miss her."

"Yes, ma'am. I just love this place and helping the children," I said.

"Young lady," Mr. Peterson said, as I shook his hand, "We want to continue the program. We'll talk to our lawyer to draw up a lease for you."

"That would be great." Mrs. Peterson handed me a little notebook where I scribbled my contact information down and handed it back to her.

Mr. Peterson glanced at the page. "Excellent. Look for an email tomorrow with the contract and lease."

My head already was spinning with everything I had to do. I couldn't wait to start on this adventure. I shook their hands one more time. The promise of the future never looked so exciting.

FIVE DAYS LATER, MY phone buzzed as I was jogging down the sidewalk after a long night at the ER. I fumbled with my water bottle until I was able to get the phone out of my pocket. The screen said, UNKNOWN CALLER. I hit the answer button on the sixth ring.

"Hello, this is Delilah Allen."

"Hello, dear this is Mrs. Peterson. How are you doing this blessed morning?" Her Texas drawl came through the phone.

"I'm good. How are you?"

"Just fine, dear. I wanted to call and talk to you about the riding stable."

"I sent back the signed lease and I mailed you the deposit a couple of days ago...Did you not get it?" My heart pounded in my chest as my breath came in short puffs. I tried to control my breathing so as not to be panting on the phone.

"Yes dear, we received your check this morning with the mail."

I leaned against the side of a brick building. The blood pounded in my ears for a totally different reason than that I was out jogging. "Okay," I said hesitantly.

"The thing is that we got an offer from a developer for that tiny bit of land, and we just can't refuse his offer."

The thudding in my head increased as I processed her words. The sun beat down warming my already warm face. "But what about the stables, the horses, and the children?" I asked.

"Well, honey, we are going to return your check and void the contract. As for the horses, they are Leah's problem. She has a month to move them. I've got to go. Bye, dear."

The phone went dead in my ear as I continued to stand there. Now what? I had already closed out my retirement to have enough money to buy the horses. They weren't Leah's problem anymore; they were my problem, too. I had given my two-weeks' notice at the hospital and going back to request to stay made me sick thinking about it. And the children and the horses. There wasn't anywhere else in San Antonio for them to get those experiences. I shuffled my way over to a bus bench as I dialed Leah's number.

"Hey, Delilah." Her voice cracked when she answered the phone on the first ring. "I was expecting your call."

"I just finished talking to Mrs. Peterson. So, it's true?" I twirled the end of my ponytail. I heard her sigh on the other end.

"Yep, and I don't know what to do. I'll return your money because I know you don't have a place for them. A month isn't long enough to find the horses good homes and I don't want to see them end up on the kill truck."

I shuddered at the thought of old Billy's greying muzzle poking through the slants on the truck, heading for a long drive to Mexico, confused as to why he was packed on a trailer with strange horses.

"No, we can't have that." I agreed.

"What are we going to do?" She cried into the phone, the sadness and despair clear in her voice. "I can't take them with me. We have a small house and no funds to care for ten horses. I'm going to have to sell them at an auction."

"Can you give me a week to figure something out before you do that?"

"Do you think you could find homes for them?" Her voice pleaded with a touch of hope.

"I hope so," I said before disconnecting. Hopefully, inspiration would strike, and I could save those horses, get a new job, and help the children; otherwise, the horses would be sold, I'd be stuck in my burnt-out career, and the kids would have nowhere to ride.

# Chapter 4 August 11th

# Kade

My backside ached. That was a new development in the last week since the accident and the reconstructive surgery to fix my shattered leg. I tallied my aches and pains: my leg hurt, breathing hurt, sitting hurt, and any moving at all left me breathless for several minutes. At least, the headache went away and so did the blurry vision. Dr. Glanders, my orthopedic surgeon, said the broken bones would take eight weeks to heal, the reconstructive surgery on my ligaments would take sixteen weeks, and my ribs would be at least eight weeks. It was going to be a long recovery, and I hated every moment of my current situation. I rang the little bell beside my recliner and waited for what seemed like forever until a little Hispanic woman bustled into my room.

"I needed you ten minutes ago," I growled and she cringed away from me. The black mood that controlled me rejoiced in her fear. "This chair is uncomfortable. Bring me a different one."

She nodded as she backed out of the room. The darkness of the room settled on my soul. The docs said I wouldn't be ready to ride at the Bull Riding Finals in November, if ever again. Three months away from living my dream, the accumulation of all the years of scratching it out in dirty hotels, poor arenas, and long days on the road. One ride and everything was torn away from me. I threw my glass of water against the wall. The glass shattered with a loud crash. The door whipped open and slammed against the wall. Kaleb's large frame blocked out the light from the hallway.

"What's going on in here?" He demanded. His eyes roved from me to the fragments glittering on the floor. "Was that necessary?"

"The woman has not brought me a new chair."

"All of this over your butt hurting." He stalked closer to me. His brows pulled down over his eyes. "The family's bull riding golden boy throws a fit when his backside hurts so much that he has to smash things like a two-year-old."

"It's uncomfortable." I ground out.

"Deal with it." He turned to go.

"Is she bringing another chair?"

"No, she quit." He tossed over his shoulder before leaving the room.

I swore under my breath. My body rocked from cheek to cheek, seeking comfort. I slouched and tried to sit up straight. No relief was found. I grabbed a couple of pain killers, swallowing them dry. The glow from the TV dimly lit the room as cowboys rode their horses across the screen. My eyelids got heavy, and I reclined back into the chair, drifting off to sleep.

The house was quiet when I woke back up. The TV was still playing. This time, John Wayne raced through a field shooting off rifles in each hand like the legend he was. I straightened in my chair, grimacing as the pain came back. My neck cricked with the way I fell asleep. I rolled my neck and shoulder, gently, trying to work out the tension. My bladder begged to be empty, but there was no way I was calling Kaleb. He would do his big brother thing and make sure I knew how much I needed him, which I did not. I could go by myself without help from anyone.

I stretched to reach my crutches because the emasculating wheelchair sat in the corner, out of reach. I couldn't get to it if I wanted to. With each armrest firmly tucked against my body, I took a step. The pain. It shot through me, leaving black spots covering my vision. My chest clenched as I drew in a ragged breath. I gritted my teeth and kept going. Step. Hop. Step. Hop. I was going to do it. Step. I swung the crutches forward.

The foot of one crutch hit the water still on the floor. As I transferred my weight forward from my good leg, the crutch slid out to the side. The next moment, I was sitting in a puddle of water. My boxers were soaked, my side hurt, and my legs pointed in opposite directions. The darkness spun around me as I tried to breathe through the pain. One breath in. One breath out. Grimacing, I repositioned my legs so I wasn't doing the splits anymore, and I pushed up with my hands, but I couldn't balance on my one good leg. I didn't have the strength to get my body up as pain coursed through me. With a sigh of defeat, I laid back down.

I didn't know how long I was like that before the door swung open in my room. A sliver of light fell across my eyes, causing me to shield them from the bright light.

"What are you doing on the floor?" Kaleb towered over me.

"Having a tea party. Wanna join?"

"Not particularly." He wheeled the chair over to me. Grasping me at the armpits, he hoisted me into the chair. "You could've called."

"Didn't want to bother you." The sarcastic tone colored my words.

"You can just say you're sorry." He muttered as he pushed the chair out of the room. "And maybe, 'thanks for taking care of me, big brother.'" The chair rolled down the hardwood floors. One of the wheels squeaked. "I've had to give up things to help you."

"Thank you, Kaleb." What else could I say to that?

He grunted in response. "Use your chair next time."

I hated that chair.

# Chapter 5 August 15th

## Delilah

The rest of the week passed uneventfully as Leah and I tried to come up with ideas for the horses and children. I was still drawing a blank when my best friend, Melanie Baker, invited me over to her fiancé's ranch to help them put up hay for the cattle.

Melanie and I were in the hayloft of the barn stacking the hay as my older brother, Damien, threw the bales onto an elevator to bring them to us from the trailer; while, Pete, the fiancé, brought in full wagons from the field.

*The children and the horses, what was I going to do?* I only had a couple more days before Leah had to put them up for sale, and then I could say goodbye to my dream of running the stable. My internal thoughts ran on repeat with no new solutions.

"Earth to Delilah!" Melanie called. A hay bale toppled off the elevator and almost hit my head. Startled, I picked up the bale and carried it to the end of the line we were stacking. Melanie stood with her hands on her hips. Old, tattered jeans and a baggy T-shirt replaced the fashionable clothes that she usually wore. Her brown hair was tucked up under a hat and her face was devoid of make-up. We'd been best friends since college, and she moved to Sunnydale a couple of months ago after she lost her job in New York City. She ended up reopening the dress shop in town and falling in love with

Pete Thompson, Damien's best friend. Country life agreed with her and she was happier than she had been in years.

"What's up with you?" She realigned the bale I'd just put down. "You've been in Lala land all afternoon, and I'm totally beating you in the number of bales being stacked." She took a swig of her water bottle, waving the tally book in her hand before continuing, "Especially, since I'm a city girl and you grew up doing this." The taunt was nothing new. Ever since she moved to Sunnydale, Texas from New York City, Melanie teased me about her becoming a country girl while I stayed in San Antonio.

"A lot on my mind," I muttered as yet another bale fell from the elevator.

"Well, tell me about it." She faked a southern drawl while hoisting the bale to its spot.

"Remember how we talked about Happy Hearts Therapeutic Riding Center?"

She nodded.

I went on to tell her about Happy Hearts Therapeutic Riding Center and my dreams for it.

"But now I have to figure out what to do with the horses within the next couple of days, otherwise, Leah is going to have to sell them." I took a cool drink from my water bottle, wiping the sweat from my brow. "I have enough money to buy them, but I don't have anywhere to keep them. And once I do have them, I'll have to beg for my job back at the ER because I won't be able to feed them."

Melanie stood with her hands on her hips, waving her hand at me to continue as bales piled up next to her as they fell off the elevator.

# SECOND CHANCE WITH MY BULL RIDER 37

"Plus, the children. I'd never be able to afford to buy a place to run the stable out of, and it brings happiness to their lives that they don't have." I sighed in frustration.

Melanie was about to say something when Damien called up, "Are you girls stacking those bales or painting your nails?"

"Stop the elevator and come up here. Your baby sister has a problem that she hasn't been sharing with anyone." She narrowed her eyes at me in mock condemnation. The whirling of the motor stopped and the elevator ground to a squeaky halt. Melanie and I quickly stacked the fallen bales while Damien climbed the ladder.

While perched on the scratchy hay bales, Melanie and I recapped my problem for Damien. He pulled out a long stalk of hay and chewed on it thoughtfully. My big brother was a retired Marine and he never faced a problem without a game plan. His muscles in his arms bunched as he straightened a few bales out.

"Oh! I know, why don't we keep the horses here for a little bit." Melanie jumped up from her hay bale. "I'm sure Pete won't mind. His cows aren't calving until January, so you have a few months yet."

I mulled that over. "That would buy me some time." I watched Damien pace back and forth across the bales. He never fell between them once. I couldn't do that; I stepped between them all the time.

"Why don't you ask Mr. Giffery to help you?" He muttered as he sat next to me. "He loves you, Dee, and I bet he'd like that idea too."

I rolled my eyes at the nickname. Damien and his friends have been calling me 'Dee' since I was little and couldn't pronounce Delilah. It was kind of cute in a way.

"You think he would help?" Hope blossomed in my chest. I knew Mr. Giffery for most of my life. He had a large ranch outside of town, next to the Kisment ranch. Damien and I used to pick up odd jobs for Mr. Giffery when we were in middle school. Painting fence posts, stacking hay, mowing his yard, washing windows on his house. He was gruff and a little scary to young children with his shaggy beard and the way he would frown down on me when I'd do silly things; until, I realized that he was very lonely on his ranch without any family around. Mr. Giffery was like a grandfather to us. He taught us how to ride, make hay, fish, and swim in his ponds. He had his own grandchildren, but they lived in Dallas and never came to visit.

"I do. He has that big barn that is empty now since he sold most of his horses. His cattle won't bother anyone since he keeps them out to pasture all the time. If that doesn't work, you can always ask Kaleb Kisment to help you."

I wrinkled my nose at that. The Kisments were the kind of people that would give you the shirts off their backs, and at one time, I considered them family. But after the break-up with Kade and losing the baby, things were never the same. I couldn't ask them for help unless it was my last option.

Damien leaned back and closed his eyes. "Now if you girls don't mind, I'm going to take a nap before the boss man gets back from the fields."

I bounced on the balls of my feet. I thought about the big barn at Mr. Giffery's place and the indoor area. "I'll be right back," I called to Melanie, climbing down to the ground floor of the barn.

"Where are you going?" She stuck her head down the ladder.

"Gotta call Mr. Giffery." I sprinted to the house to call him on the landline; maybe, this was the answer to my prayers.

# SECOND CHANCE WITH MY BULL RIDER

I PULLED ON THE SLEEVES of my steel grey suit. It was uncomfortable and foreign. I was used to wearing scrubs, workout clothes, or jeans and T-shirts. It pinched in my stomach and was restrictive across my shoulders. Glancing at myself in my bathroom mirror, I brushed my long black hair until it was untangled and shiny. I dug through my makeup bag to find my plum lipstick. It would match the pinstripes on my suit. My hand shook as I raised it to my lips; the lower lid applied smoothly. I was halfway through my upper lip when my phone buzzed. I jumped. "Now there is lipstick everywhere!" I dabbed at the wayward color as I read the message.

**Melanie: I'm outside of your apartment. Time to go!!!! ?**

I put on the final touches of makeup before hurrying out the door and down my apartment steps to meet Melanie.

"Are you ready?" She asked as I slid into her red car. Her knuckles turned white as they gripped the steering wheel. The car moved swiftly through traffic. San Antonio traffic wasn't like driving in New York City.

"Thank you for coming with me." I twisted a lock of hair before tucking it behind my ear. "I'm nervous to go by myself. I don't have any business experience."

"That's what friends are for. It's no big deal. Just a meeting with Mr. Giffery and the loan officer. If it's Mr. Dillard, he's not so bad. He gave me a loan for the dress shop."

I nodded as she parked in front of a swanky coffee shop in San Antonio where Mr. Giffery and the loan officer sat by a window overlooking the street. Mr. Giffery had a large cowboy hat that shaded his blue eyes that crinkled in the corners when he saw me. He rose as I approached the table to wrap me in a bear hug.

"Dee, my dear. I haven't seen you in years." He beamed down at me and held me at arm's length. "You have grown up so much. I almost didn't recognize you in a suit."

"I don't recognize myself in a suit, either."

His deep booming laugh settled into my bones and brought back memories of fishing with him and horseback riding; even though, he looked foreign with a tailored suit covering his sinewy body.

"This must be Melanie Baker. Nice to meet you, young lady. I've heard about all the good things you are doing for Elizabeth's old dress shop" He shook her hand with both of his. Melanie's cheeks stained a bright pink.

"Thank you. Without Miss Elizabeth or the rest of the Thompsons, I wouldn't have a business." Pete's aunt, Miss Elizabeth, owned the old dress shop that Melanie had renovated to Chic Designs by Mel. She designed high-end fashion, costumes, prom dresses, and wedding dresses.

"This is Mr. Dillard, my loan officer. I'd like him to be in on this meeting." Mr. Giffery gestured to the other man at the table.

Mr. Dillard rose to shake both of our hands. The handshake was weak and clammy. He looked down his bulbous nose at us. "Nice to meet, y'all." His chins wiggled as he spoke. His suit hung open on either side of his ample belly.

We settled into the table as a waitress came to take our drink orders. Mr. Dillard also ordered two giant muffins. He ate the muffins with crumbs falling onto his stomach and table. Melanie and Mr. Giffery sipped their coffee, and I rocked my cup back and forth. The foam dissolved into the dark liquid. My belly clenched and rolled, mocking the movements of my cup. Sweat accumulated under my suit and my palms went clammy. Mr. Dillard licked his fingers before wiping them on the napkin.

"Dee," Mr. Giffery said. "Did you ever make up with the youngest Kisment boy?"

Next to me, Melanie slurped a large gulp of coffee and stilled, watching me. Her eyes were as big as saucers. My throat was suddenly dry, and I swallowed several times.

"No," I answered quietly.

"That's too bad. You were a cute couple and would've made beautiful babies." His eyes were sad when I met them.

Unconsciously, my hand fell to my lower abdomen and rubbed it for a second. "Yes." My voice broke. "It would have been a true love story." An awkward silence fell over the table as everyone watched me. My mind wanted to wander back eleven years to the summer after my senior year. Mentally shaking myself, I cleared my throat and opened the folder I brought with me.

"Let's talk about your therapeutic riding stable." Mr. Giffery directed his statement at me, watching my hands stack the papers in front of me.

"I want to take over the therapeutic riding stable in San Antonio and have Melanie become my partner. It's closing soon, and all the children that use it will be left without a place to ride. It helps them by stimulating muscles that they don't normally use, and it is also good for their mental health. I've secured the horses currently being used in the program, but we need a facility to house and run the program out of. We also need to buy or rent this list of equipment." I handed out the documents that we'd prepared, a copy for both men.

"This is our projected expenses and income. We broke it down by monthly and yearly." Melanie handed another stack of papers to Mr. Dillard.

Mr. Dillard read over the papers and then looked at us. "How much do you need for startup costs?"

Melanie and I glanced at each other. "We estimate about $75,000 for costs and to pay rent for the property for the year."

Mr. Dillard grunted before going back over the numbers. "Do you have any money for a down payment?"

"No, sir. We were looking for a loan to cover it." Melanie explained.

Mr. Dillard grunted, again, and frowned at us. "That could be a problem. The bank has a policy to loan money to only low-risk investments. I'm afraid that this would not be one."

Melanie and I shared a look. My heart fell at his words. *What were we going to do?*

Mr. Giffery crossed his arms and leaned back in his chair. "I have a solution." We swiveled our heads to look at him. "I'd like to donate $25,000 to the cause and you would be able to rent my barn free of charge."

"That would bring the amount you need for the loan down quite a bit." Mr. Dillard chewed on the last piece of muffin.

"I also would like to co-sign the loan."

My jaw dropped as I bounced in my seat. *Would he really? How exciting!* Melanie's face had the same expression of shock.

"That should help with the loan papers." Mr. Giffery smiled happily at me. "I just want to help out my girl."

I leaped from the table and ran around it to give him a big hug. He chuckled as he patted me awkwardly on the back.

"Thank you, Mr. Giffery! That will help the kids so much," I said. Emotion clogged my throat. I pulled away from him, and he handed me a handkerchief when tears leaked out of my eyes and streamed down my face.

"No crying. You know what tears do to an old man," he said, his eye shone in excitement.

Mr. Dillard calculated the numbers while we sat in silence. "The bank might be able to give you the loan. I must run it by the board first, of course. But I don't see how they can object if Mr. Giffery is helping you out." He patted his abdomen again and wiped crumbs from his fingers.

---

IT WAS A BEAUTIFUL day. Most days in August in San Antonio were. The sun shone, birds sang, and kids played at the local park. I completed my run and stopped at the local coffee shop to get my favorite iced mocha when my phone let out a few buzzes. Melanie's name popped up on the screen.

"Hi, Melanie. What's up?" I answered as I slurped a big gulp of chocolatey, coffee goodness. "I thought we were meeting in a little bit?"

"We were, but this is too pressing to wait until you get here." Panic edged in her voice causing my stomach to drop. Melanie was usually unflappable, and I have only seen her breakdown one time. That was before she met her fiancé, Pete.

"Ok." Another slurp, and a rattle of ice.

"I just heard from Pete who heard from someone that Mr. Giffery died this morning."

"What!" The plastic cup half full of coffee hit the ground splattering my yoga pants and tennis shoes. My stomach dropped and the noise of the outside world faded to just me and Melanie. *We were supposed to meet him today. Oh no! Had he been sick? What happened? What did that mean for us?*

"Delilah, are you still there?"

I nodded my head, even if she couldn't see me. "Yes." I croaked while I leaned back against the stone wall of a building.

"From what Pete found out, the doctors are saying that he had a heart attack. Stella, his housekeeper, found him."

Again, I nodded. I knew Stella. She had been taking care of Mr. Giffery and his house for decades. That poor woman. Tears coursed down my cheeks in hot tracks, dripping off the end of my nose as a sniffle rose.

"I don't know much else," Melanie said. "It's going to take a while for his family to get back into town. I think this puts our plans on hold for the moment."

"His money-hungry children," I groaned. "They were always too busy to help him with the ranch. And now that he is gone. Who knows what they will want to do with it?"

"I know but worrying about it is not going to help us. Why don't we meet up this afternoon at my house to go over the plans?"

I agreed and hung up. Even though the sun was still shining, and it was still a beautiful day, a dark cloud hung over my head. Sadness beat in my heart and a small bit of panic raced through me. I jogged my way home in coffee-stained clothes and wet shoes.

I drove my black Jetta the thirty miles into Sunnydale that afternoon to meet Melanie at her and Pete's ranch-style house on the edge of town. Only Melanie's little Honda was parked in the drive when I pulled up. I gathered my papers into a pile and unfolded myself out of the car. Melanie opened the door before I knocked, looking lovely in a red flowing shirt and white shorts. Her hair was cut in the latest fashion and make-up was perfectly done. I tugged at my T-shirt and tried to straighten my wild ponytail. Her lips quirked into a half-grin.

"I have been offering to show you how to do your hair for years, ever since that boy liked you in college."

I blushed a bit, remembering how awkward I was back then. "No, I'm good."

She swung the door open to let me walk in. Pete's house was the quintessential bachelor pad before he met Melanie. Now, local artists' works hung on the walls, plush couches were in the living room, and the fridge was full of food. She led the way to the small, bright kitchen and pulled out some lemonade. She was from New York and didn't care for sweet tea.

"Would you like some?"

"Sure, Pete must be gaining weight from all that food in there." I glanced inside to see leftover casserole, veggies, and chicken thawing for tonight. He was lucky to have milk and some bread before Melanie came along. She laughed. Then, she settled at the table and started up her laptop.

"Let's think worst-case scenario. What if we don't get the money Mr. Giffery was going to donate?" She unclicked some buttons in the spreadsheet she was working on. The bottom number went from black to a bright red. She grabbed a pencil and twirled it while she contemplated the number at the bottom. My heart dropped as I had sunk into the chair next to her.

"That's a lot of money." I felt numb. $25,000 was a lot of money; plus, we'd have to find another place to rent and another co-signer. With his help, it would have gotten us off the ground and be sustainable by the second year of business.

"We're back at the drawing board, aren't we?" I tapped my foot absently against the stool.

Melanie nodded, "We'd have to start over with everything, the loan for the bank, funding for the feed, building, land, and everything else."

I placed my head in my hands. I wanted to bang my head against a wall, but I knew it wouldn't help. The little bit of panic that was inside of me before grew and spread throughout my body. Tremors coursed down my arms and legs and my chest contracted painfully.

"At least, we still have our jobs. We can save the money until we have enough to bring before the bank for a loan." Melanie sipped from her lemonade, staring at the screen.

"You still have your job." I groaned and tried to breathe out slowly. "I gave my two-week notice last week, and I don't really want to beg for it back! I hate it there!" Melanie gasped and I couldn't meet her eyes. "After we met with Mr. Giffery and everything was set to go through with the bank, I guess I jumped the gun." I shrugged and dragged my fingers across the seam in the table.

"I was wondering how you got so much done working third shift." A little chuckle came from her. "I thought you were superwoman. Never sleeping."

"No, I'm just a dumb woman who quits her job prematurely." I scoffed. I stole a chocolate chip cookie from the plate in the middle of the table. "The hospital has a no rehire policy, but I guess I could try to find another job."

I cringed. I was burnt out in the emergency room. There were only so many car accidents, sick people, and midnight shifts this girl could take. Not only that, I was broke. After buying the horses,

I had enough money to cover my rent payment for next month and that was it.

"I was ready for our therapeutic riding stable to be up and running. I don't want to be a nurse anymore." Tears threatened to fill my eyes for everything: the loss of Mr. Giffery, the potential loss of our riding stable, the children that need our help, and, lastly, my lack of employment.

Melanie wrapped me in a hug and rubbed my back. "We will figure this out."

---

"SO, YOU SEE, MIKE, we need to raise money to fund the therapeutic riding stable." Melanie pointed to the presentation we brought with us to Mike's Auto Shop on the corner of Main Street and Highway 4 in Sunnydale. It was a gas station and a fix-it shop. "With your donation, we will be able to provide an experience that will help these children." I paced behind Mike as Melanie finished. She had more experience in fundraising money for things than I did. She came from old money in New York where her mother raised money for a charity like it was as easy as painting toenails. I was a simple country girl, in comparison.

Mike tossed the towel over his shoulder before stuffing his hands in the pockets of his coveralls. He leaned against the counter with his belly starting to get the middle age pouch. "I'd love to help you gals out, but it has been a hard year for me...I can donate a fifty." He rifled through his cash register and pulled out a bill, handing it to Melanie. Her face fell slightly at the sight, but she quickly put a bright smile on. She was that good.

"That's nice of you, Mike." She took the fifty and wrote him out a receipt. "We'll put your name on the donor board."

A smile creased Mike's grease-covered face. "Can't wait to see the place." He enveloped both of us in a bear hug, before heading back to work on a car.

Melanie pocketed the cash and I picked up the poster board. She looked about as sad as I felt.

She slid the presentation in the back seat of her car. "I was hoping for something better." She sat in the driver's seat and softly shut the door.

"We've hit Cowboy's Bar, the bank, the veterinary clinic, Sunny's Flowers and Gifts, Betty's Better Cuts, and now Mike's Auto." I checked them off on the sheet. "How much did we raise?"

"$394.75" She added up her receipt book. I blew out a sigh.

"That only leaves Susie's Café, the new coffee shop, and S.D. Manufacturing to ask," I said, ticking the places off on my fingers.

"Pete's already asked at the factory. They have a no donation policy." Melanie tucked a stray hair behind her ears.

"Bummer, I am not hopeful for the coffee shop, but let's go ask. It's hard being a new business."

"I know that." Melanie laughed dryly. Her dress shop had been open for a couple of months, and it was in the black most months, but that was mainly due to Melanie's talent and contacts all over the country.

I chewed on my nails while Melanie drove us across the street to the brand-new coffee shop and bakery. It opened the week before, and the rumor mill said her muffins were heavenly.

A small bell tinkled as we pushed through the glass door. The scent of fresh-baked blueberry muffins filled the air. Coffee machines percolated on the back counter. A tiny woman with spiky blue hair stood on a stool behind the glass display filled with pastry.

"Good morning, darlin'. What can I help you with?" She drawled in a thick southern accent.

"I'm Melanie Baker and this is my friend Delilah Allen." Melanie extended a manicured hand over the case to clasp the woman's equally manicured hand.

"Oh yes, you own that darlin' dress shop a couple of blocks down." She stepped off the stool and made her way around the counter. "I'm Viola Ann. I just moved here from Georgia." She shook my hand too. Her nails were painted a bright red with little white cupcakes on them. I glanced at my chewed ones and hid them behind my back.

"I could do with a chocolate mocha," I said, "I need the caffeine." I shrugged at Melanie's look.

Melanie scanned the whiteboard where the specials were listed. "I'll have a triple berry scone."

Viola Ann started to make the mocha and warm the scone up.

"We were wondering if you would like to donate to our therapeutic riding stable." I blurted out.

Viola Ann stopped building the mocha. "Oh, honey, I would love to. But I sunk everything I had into this little place." She shrugged and glanced around. "It's not easy to be a bakery."

My face burned as I stared at my toes. Melanie gave me a 'what was that?' look. Viola Ann brought out the mocha and the scone, and we gave her our money before retreating to the car.

"What are we going to do?" Melanie closed the car door behind her. She bit into her scone, groaning for a moment. "This is heavenly." She said around a mouth full of pastry. I sipped my mocha, waiting for her to continue. It was delicious, a rich chocolatey coffee with just the right amount of foam. It tickled my upper lip, leaving a little mustache. Melanie burst out laughing.

She reached over and handed me a napkin from the glove compartment. She motioned to my face. I took it and dabbed at it.

"Seriously what are we going to do?" I tried not to wail, but our situation was getting bleak.

"Have you heard from Mr. Giffery's lawyer?" Melanie asked.

"He didn't have anything about the riding stable in his will. That's not at all that surprising." I twisted a strand of hair around my fingers. "I mean we have only been discussing it for a few days, and he wasn't expecting to die. According to the lawyer, his children are going to auction off the ranch and split the money between them."

"Bummer. The shop is barely making a profit this month. I don't have any spare cash. And I'm not asking my parents for help." She blew her bangs out of her eyes. Melanie spent her whole life being under her parents' control and money. Now that she lived in Sunnydale, she was determined to make her own way in life. "Do you have any ideas?"

"What about asking Pete if we could rent a little space from him, just to get started?" I swirled my cup around, mixing in the chocolate that settled on the bottom.

"I'll ask again. But he is worried about the liability of having children around his bucking bull cows. They aren't the tamest things in the world."

I snorted. "No kidding." The week before, the UPS truck scared them, and they ran through a fence. Not something I wanted to happen with a bunch of kids with special needs and their families hanging around. "That's understandable. Maybe another place will come along. We do need to get the money problem straightened out first. Otherwise, it doesn't matter how tame Pete's cows aren't."

Melanie laughed at that; while I thought of little Tabitha in her wheelchair and how happy the horses made her and how much help this could be. A pit formed in my stomach. I had to do this, anyway I can.

"I will donate all of my savings." What little I have, I thought. "But I may need a place to stay for a while." Heat rose to my cheeks as Melanie started the car, not looking at me. A heavy silence filled the car.

She pulled into a parking spot in front of Susie's Café. "You can stay at my place. I am not using the little apartment above the dress shop for anything."

The bell rang over our heads as we made our way into the café. It was one of those quaint places that had a long counter running the length with booths on the other side. Susie had her grey hair pulled up in a bun with a hairnet over it, flipping burgers on the grill for a couple of customers sitting at the counter. We each took a stool and flipped through the menu. Lindsay came sashaying over, pouring coffee for the older men next to us.

"Good morning, girls," she purred. "What could I start you with today? Sweet tea, Dee, and lemonade for you, Melanie?"

"That would be good." Melanie frowned as I laughed at her.

"Having a hard time getting used to being in a small town where everyone knows your business?" I joked, adding more sugar to my sweet tea.

"Oh, honey, everyone here knows you don't drink sweet tea seeing as you're a Yank." Lindsay turned and grabbed the burgers from Susie to give to the other customers.

"Susie, if you have a minute, could we talk to you?" I called as she started to head back to her office.

"Sure, girls." She wiped her hands on her once white apron before leaning on the counter. "What can I do for you?"

Melanie launched into the spiel that she had been giving all morning. Susie listened until the end.

"That sounds wonderful, but all I can donate is a hundred dollars." She went to her office and came back with a large bill which she handed to Melanie before walking away.

Melanie and I shared a glance before sipping our drinks. This was going to be a tough uphill battle if we were to raise the money for at least the down payment.

"What y'all doing with the horses?" Lindsay topped off our drinks before pulling out an order book.

I shrugged. "I was hoping to sweet talk Pete into letting me keep them at his ranch."

Lindsay wrinkled her nose. "But he has all those rodeo cows. Not good for little children." She wrinkled her nose as she chewed on the end of her pencil. "We have room at my uncle's place for some horses. How many did you say there were?"

"Seriously! That would be awesome," I squealed and jumped out of my seat to hug her over the counter. "There is ten total."

She blushed and tucked a blond curl behind her ear, nodding. "Well, you've helped me out a time or two. Burgers are okay?" She walked to the refrigerator to get beef patties. Lindsay could be standoffish, and we were never the best of friends, but she has not had an easy life. Neighbors watch out for one another in a small town.

"That takes a little pressure off." Melanie sipped on her lemonade. "Just got to get the money."

HAPPY HEARTS THERAPEUTIC Riding Center was eerily quiet. Leah walked down the barn aisle saying her good-byes to the horses. No children, parents, or other volunteers were there; it was just the two of us. All the saddles and bridles had been moved to Pete's ranch where he had a large barn. Leah was whispering to Billy, the old Percheron cross, when Pete's truck and trailer pulled into the drive. He drove up to the barn, swung it around, and backed it up to the door. Melanie jumped out of the passenger side and hurried around to open the back gate of the long stock trailer.

Leah came over to me, with her eyes shining with unshed tears. She wrapped me in a hug, and I hugged her back.

"You have no idea how much this means to me," she said when she stepped out of our embrace. "Not to see the horses going to an auction."

"I know, my heart hurts just thinking about that." I glanced over my shoulder to see all their heads over the stall doors, ears perked toward the trailer. I reached into my back pocket and pulled out the check for all the horses. It was folded in half when I slipped it into her hand.

"I can't take this," Leah stared at the check. "I wasn't expecting you to pay me."

"We'd talked about it and you need the money for moving." I shrugged.

"What about you?" Her eyes searched mine. "Didn't you quit your job?"

"It will be fine," I said, even if I didn't believe it myself.

Melanie strode over to us and swung her arm around my shoulders. "Besides, she's moving back to Sunnydale, and her landlord isn't charging her rent."

Leah raised her eyebrows at me as I blushed and looked at my feet.

"I'm moving into the apartment above Melanie's shop. She's not living there anymore, and rent is a lot cheaper than in San Antonio."

"Yeah, free." Melanie laughed when Pete came into the stable.

"Ready to load them up?" He grabbed a lead rope from the front of the first stall and clipped it to Jasper, a bay Quarter Horse gelding. Leah nodded and hurried over to the next horse.

All ten of the horses were loaded and Leah fed them apple slices one more time. We were on the road to Lindsay's place. She and her mother lived with her uncle for years on the Wilson family ranch, which sat outside of Sunnydale. The thirty-minute drive flew by as I followed the truck and trailer in my Jetta.

Pete swung the truck and trailer into the driveway and continued under the large wooden sign with Flying W burnt into it. It was faded and peeling since I last was here in high school. We followed the drive up to a double-wide with a small deck and ramp leading to the front door. The long, dead grass filled what used to be a trimmed lawn and bushes grew wild along the side of the trailer. Pete pulled up to the barn, which was leaning to one side with a split rail fence running the edge of a pasture. Lindsay waved to us where she was clearing tall grass away from the gate. Pete pulled up and killed the engine as I drove next to him. The screen door slammed as Lindsay's mother rolled her wheelchair to the deck.

"Hi, Miss Wilson," Pete greeted her by removing his cowboy hat.

"Nonsense, stop calling me that." She waved him away. "There is homemade ice cream in the freezer when y'all are done with those horses." She caught my eye. "Nice to see you home, Dee."

"That it is, Miss Wilson."

She shook her head and turned her wheelchair around to the house.

We unloaded the horses into the pasture where Lindsay was fixing the gate. They ran around, tossing their heads, and bucking before settling down to graze. I leaned my elbows against the rough planks and watched them. Lindsay stood on one side and Melanie on the other side of me. Pete went inside to get some of Miss Wilson's homemade ice cream.

"There wasn't any pasture in San Antonio," I said. Penny ran circles around Billy, and he laid his ears back at her.

"I think they'll enjoy it here." Lindsay popped her gum. "We have a lot of pasture that ain't being used."

"Did your uncle say how much board is?" I worried about my bank account.

"He said to just chip in for hay if they're here that long." Lindsay rested a boot on the lower plank. The horses spooked at something and lapped around the field. "We've plenty of hay too. We only have a couple of cows and my ancient horse left." Her voice sounded sad. I glanced over at her, but she avoided my gaze, twirling a long piece of grass between her fingers.

"Well, tell him thank you from the bottom of my heart."

Lindsay smiled and nodded. Jasper trotted up and blew snot over all of us. I laughed wiping my face with the back of my hand. At least my horses were going to be alright. I had a temporary place to live; now, I just needed to find a job.

# Chapter 6 September 1st

## Delilah

I pushed my cart up the frozen food aisle at the little grocery store in Sunnydale. It was so small; I could walk the whole store in ten minutes. What I needed right now was comfort food. With my last five-dollar bill burning that proverbial hole in my pocket, I stared at the ice cream selection. I moved closer to the glass as another cart approached. The wheels squeaked with each turn. It stopped right next to me. I glanced over my shoulder, staring directly into the dark blue eyes of Kaleb Kisment. I had known him for years, ever since I was little. Every girl in town went gooey when he smiled, but it did nothing for me. I knew him too well. I knew his family too well. And every girl knew not to date the big brother of your ex-boyfriend, no matter how cute he was or how nice his parents were.

"Hi, Dee." His deep voice rumbled. He leaned against his cart, observing the display.

"Hi, Kaleb, am I in your way?" I scooted to the side so he could contemplate the ice cream, too. His cart was filled with food: frozen dinners, frozen pizza, snack cakes, and loads of sports drinks. That was a lot of food for a single man.

"What brings you to Sunnydale to shop?" He picked a couple of cartons of mint chocolate chip. The cold air from the freezer blasted into the aisle, raising goosebumps up my arms.

"I live here now."

His eyebrows raised, and he glanced into my empty cart.

"I'm staying in the apartment above the dress shop." I waved my hands around like that was no big deal. *It wasn't, was it?* "It's nice to be living back in the hometown. San Antonio was too busy, too many people, trains, and planes."

A half grin cocked his mouth.

"You're enjoying the commute for your job, though?" It was stated but held a tiny bit of question in it.

"Um," I looked at my shoes. My face heated up and the tips of my ears felt like they were on fire. "I am kind of in-between jobs right now. Just going with the flow." Shrugging, I met his gaze straight on with a red face.

Kaleb went back to choosing ice cream bars. My throat closed when he picked up four boxes of the cookie ice cream sandwiches. They were Kade's favorite ice cream. A pang of longing hit deep within me. I wondered what he was doing and where he was. Was he O.K? I hadn't seen him since he was in San Antonio earlier this summer for the bull riding.

"Would you like a temporary job?" He turned back, haphazardly piling the boxes on top of the sports drinks.

"Depends on what it is." I twirled the end of my ponytail around my fingers. *What could he offer me? Should I bring up the therapeutic riding stable?*

"Well, I'd offer you a stall cleaning job, but I hired a couple of new guys last week. How would you like something that pays a little better and is in your skillset?" His eyes narrowed and his brows pulled down as he watched me.

"I'm listening." I leaned on my cart only to have it roll a few inches away. Stumbling, I righted myself. A smile tugged at the corners of his lips.

"Kade got seriously injured a couple of weeks ago." His deep voice rumbled.

My body betrayed my feelings. A gasp sucked in with my breath. Heart pounded harder. All the blood in my face drained away. My hands clenched into fists that I rammed into my jean's pockets. "Is he going to be O.K?" My words came out in a whisper. *Come on, Delilah. Pull yourself together. It has been years.* I hated how I still had residual feelings for him, even after all these years. Any sane person would have moved on with their lives.

Kaleb went on, ignoring my question. "I can't take care of him and the ranch at the same time. It is too much." His eyes went to a far-off place as if he were trying to do math in his head or think about a list he forgot at home. "I could use some help with Kade so I can focus on the ranch. What do you think?"

"I don't know. Kade and I aren't on speaking terms." I picked up a package of ice cream bars. *Really? He's going to ask me to take care of Kade? After our history together? After how much he hurt me?*

He seemed to consider that for a moment. "Everyone has their price, Dee. How about $10,000 for the length of his recovery?"

I scoffed at the amount. I rolled the idea around in my head. Being in the same room as Kade would be, painful, very painful. Was $10,000 going to be enough to deal with his arrogant self-centered self? I didn't think so. It was a lot of money, but not quite the amount I needed for the therapeutic riding stable, which is the only reason I would even think to do this. At least that is what I told myself.

"How long is his recovery?" I turned to face him, placing the box of ice cream in my cart.

"The doctors say six months."

I grimaced.

"What about $20,000 for the length of his recovery?" He pushed his hands through his dark blonde hair making it stand on end.

I shook my head and started to walk away. That was definitely not enough to be in Kade's presence. I could find another nursing job for that money. Maybe, I could get another job at a different hospital or teach at the university. His hand reached out and grabbed my shoulder.

"What about $50,000 for the whole recovery? If you can get him healed up and out of bed before the six months, I will give you an additional five grand."

Now, that was a lot of money. Kaleb must be desperate for help. *Could I be with Kade for his whole recovery? Where else could I make that much money? I certainly didn't make that much at the hospital. Plus, I really needed it. How horrible could it possibly be? I could ignore his arrogant comments and everything else that irritated me. That money would get the therapeutic riding stable set up. Melanie wouldn't have to ask her parents or Pete to help us.*

"How do you have that kind of money?" Crossing my arms, I met his stare. I wanted to be sure that he could pay me before I took the job. Kaleb was a rancher and notorious for being a penny pincher.

"The ranch is doing quite well, and Kurt is helping out." His blue eyes challenged me to question him further, but I didn't need to. The Kisment brothers were a tight group and took care of their own. Last I heard, Kurt, the middle brother, was a defense lawyer in Dallas and making millions of dollars. At least that is what the rumor mill at Susie's Café had said. I also heard that his firm was one of Kade's biggest sponsors.

"Fine, I will do it for fifty grand." I extended my hand, and Kaleb's big hand enclosed around mine.

"If you or Kade leave before he is released from the doctor to go back to full duty, no money. Understand?" He gave it a light squeeze.

I nodded. It shouldn't be a problem. I smirked; I could always strap him to the bed.

"Great, I'll see you this afternoon." He pushed his cart down the aisle. "Oh, Delilah. Bring your bags. You're staying at the house with us."

"What!?" I spun back towards him, but he was already walking away.

Of course. There was always the fine print with the Kisment boys.

***

A FLOOD OF MEMORIES accosted me as I turned up the dirt road to the Kisment ranch. This was where Damien and I rode horses, fished, and shot guns with the Kisment brothers and Pete. I had my first kiss on the ranch and my first heartbreak. Ma and Pa Kisment were like family to Damien and me. Once Kade walked out on me, I never went back. There were too many good memories and too much heartbreak. Plus, the Kisments were changed after that. They treated me like I was fragile, that I would break at any moment. But that was years ago...

*Come on, Delilah,* I said to myself. *Put your big girl panties on and just drive up the lane. You are over him.* I straightened my little Jetta and crept up the drive. The Kisment ranch was the biggest around. They had several thousand acres, thousands of cows, and a thriving hay business. Obviously, they did not keep up the drive as my car bounced from one pothole to another. I gritted my teeth and steered it over to the grassy side to continue my way.

The large ranch house came into view. Nothing seemed to have changed from the way it was eleven years ago, except Kaleb was the one waiting for me on the porch instead of Kade. I steered my car under the large oak tree, putting it into park. He grabbed my bags from the back seat and gave me a one-armed hug.

"Welcome home," he said as he looked over my shoulder. I followed his gaze, but there were only cows and grass behind me. Tension simmered between us as he walked me to the door. I wasn't the only one nervous about this arrangement.

"Err, thanks." I pulled back and strode to the door. Awkwardness filled me. This hadn't been my home in a long time. Did the Kisments still feel that way toward me? Swallowing against the lump in my throat, I asked "How's the patient been today?"

He held the door open so I could pass. "I'll let you see for yourself. I'll put your things in Katie's room across the hall." He shifted his weight from side to side. "You know where everything is. It hasn't changed since you were here last, so help yourself."

"No problem." I tried to sound bubbly and confident. Inside, I was quaking in my shoes. *I chose to take care of Kade Kisment. How desperate was I!*

"And Delilah." I turned toward Kaleb's voice as he made his way back outside. His dark blue eyes showed relief and a lightness he hadn't had earlier. "Thanks." The screen door screeched shut behind him.

"Yep, no problem," I muttered. I steeled myself and walked briskly from the kitchen to the wing where the bedrooms were. I set my purse and duffel bag on Katie's bed. Katie was the youngest Kisment child and only girl. With three older brothers, she girlified everything. Everything in the room was pink: pink carpet, pink walls, pink comforter, and large pink cat posters. My stomach rolled at all the pink. *It was temporary I told myself. I guess I could get used to all the pink.* Katie was a talented photographer that currently lived in Colorado with her fiancé, Levi. There was talk that they were coming home to get married and settle in Sunnydale.

Zip came trotting down the hall from another room. His stumpy tail wagged so hard his butt wiggled with excitement. He tried to jump on to my knees, but his hind legs gave out. He ended up flat on his bottom, his pink tongue rolling out of the side of his mouth.

"At least, you're happy to see me." I knelt and rubbed his ears. "It has been a long time." He groaned and kicked his back leg as I scratched his favorite spot. "We'll see if your owner is just as happy to see me."

Across the hall stood the black door that led into Kade's room. A TV droned from somewhere deep within the room. The light flickered underneath the crack in the door. "Shoulders back, chin up, stomach in," I muttered to myself. The brass knob was cold under my fingertips as it turned. The door creaked as it swung open. The light from the hall fell onto the bed. He was propped up with pillows. When our eyes met, the amount of anger and darkness in them was unexpected. My heart constricted in my chest, and there wasn't enough stale air left in the room to breathe.

"Go away." He growled as he turned to the wall.

"Well too bad." I marched across the room to the desk. His discharge instructions were strewn across the desk along with sheets from the in-home nurses and his medications. My eyes scanned the papers as I organized and filed the information away. *Boy, he did it good this time.* The springs on the bed whined as he moved.

"Go away, Delilah." His eyes burned into my back. When I turned towards him, he was perched on the edge of his bed. His skin held a sickly pallor. Dark bags circled his eyes and his blond hair stuck out at all angles. The thin t-shirt clung to his bony body. The last time I saw him was a few months ago when he had arrived with a concussion in the emergency room where I had worked. At that time, he filled out his shirt nicely with tight muscles and a flat stomach. Now, I could see his ribs through the thin fabric. The boxers ended in long skinny legs with knobby knees. His bare feet rested on a brindle cowhide. I pushed down the pity that welled in my throat. I knew Kade, and he wouldn't take pity.

"That is not going to happen." I counted out his medications. "You look like death. When was the last time you ate?"

"Thanks, but no one asked your opinion." His hands gripped the edge of the mattress, causing his knuckles to turn white.

"Take these." I thrust the pills into his face and grabbed the glass of water sitting next to him. I shook my head. "Not to keep up on your pain medications. No wonder why you hurt so bad." I muttered under my breath. I glared down at him. His icy blue eyes challenged me right back. "I have all day."

Swearing under his breath, he took the medication and swallowed it dry. "Now go away."

"Gladly" Flipping my hair over my shoulders as I left the room. "I'll check on you in a while. Get some sleep." I closed the door behind me as a pillow hit it.

# Chapter 7 September 1st

## Kade

Of all people, Delilah Allen had to be in the house. I had been avoiding her for years, ever since that day. I mentally shook myself. *Not those thoughts.* I ran into her when the circuit was in San Antonio, and I picked a mean bugger of a bull that threw me. Luckily, I only had a concussion and needed a couple of stitches. It had been fun to tease her that weekend.

The past decade had been good to her. Her long legs led up to an athletic body. She must work out all the time. Her black hair was shiny and swung down to her lower back. I forgot how beautiful her hair was. I groaned as I turned back to the wall. I didn't want her to see me like this. I was a broken-down cowboy with nothing left. My career was over. At thirty-one years old, I was one of the oldest guys on the circuit. Coming back from this injury was not likely, even the doctors thought so. I heard their whispering in the hallways outside of my hospital room. I gave everything for this career, and I have nothing to show for it. The hurt that I caused my family and friends. The family events I've missed, I can't get any of it back, and I didn't even go out with the world champion title. I have nothing.

I could hear her in the kitchen making a racket with the pots and the pans. Her lovely voice filled the quiet house with a country song as she worked at whatever she was doing in there. When she came into my bedroom, she looked like a palm tree to a man stranded in the desert. She was right I did look like death warmed over. I felt like it too. My leg hurt. It hurt to breathe. I couldn't pick anything up. I fell behind on taking my pain medication. It was easier to lay in bed than to take care of myself. Was there any point to taking care of myself? What was left of my life?

Kaleb did not have the time to care for me. He was busy running the ranch and every time he talked to me there was a bite to his words. Why did he resent me? Was I a drain on my family? The darkness of the room helped to soothe my racing, colliding thoughts as sleep overtook me. The pain was dulled by the little pills Delilah forced me to take.

A noise in my room woke me from a light sleep. The lights were turned on and blinded me. My eyelids blinked rapidly as I tried to focus on what was going on in my room. Delilah was sitting in a chair with scrambled eggs. My dormant stomach woke with a loud gurgle. She giggled while I glared at her. *How dare she walk into my bedroom without knocking to wake me up to make me eat?*

"You can pretend you're not hungry. But obviously, you are." She smothered the eggs with salsa and mixed them up. A giant fork full went into her mouth. She grinned and patted her flat stomach. "Hmmm, these are so good." She drew out the good for emphasis.

"Woman, are you going to sit there and eat?" My stomach gurgled again as she nodded. "Either share with me or leave the room." She glared at me before reaching over to the nightstand and handed me a fork. The eggs were awful; I tried not to grimace while trying to swallow a rubbery fork full, thankfully the salsa added a little spice to them and made them barely edible. But she had remembered how I liked my eggs, and I recalled how bad of a cook she was. Some things never changed. A small spot of softness melted in my heart before the rage covered it. *How dare she act like I couldn't take care of myself? What right did she have to even be here?* I jerked the plate from her and scooped some eggs in my mouth before turning back to the wall. I was starving, and I ate the rest of the plate in five mouthfuls. A look fleeted across her face before she snatched the empty plate back. My stomach rolled with the pain I caused her. But we both knew it was going to be for the best. We couldn't be together and that was that.

"You're welcome, Kade." She placed her hands on her hips and tossed her hair back. "Your ma would be ashamed of your manners."

"My ma ain't here now, is she?" I shot back.

"I'm just trying to help."

"Are you? Aren't you here to gloat? Or stick it to me? Or just torture me with your presence?" I closed my eyes and leaned against the pillows.

She was quiet for a moment, and I almost thought she left the room.

"No, I'm here to get you better. I'm the only one Kaleb thought could deal with your arrogance, pig-headedness, and general lack of manners." She glared at me. Her large brown eyes darkening with storm clouds. "It isn't always about you."

"How can this not be about me?" I shouted at her. "I'm the one in the bed! I don't need you and never will." Tears leaked out of her eyes and ran down her cheeks before she left the room. I hurt her again. That was the one thing I was an expert at.

After she left the room, the door to Katie's room slammed shut. Why would she go there? She hated pink, said it gave her monstrous headaches. I reached for my cell phone and called

Kaleb. It rang five times before he picked up. Cows bellering and the tractor running came through the earpiece.

"Please don't tell me you ran her off, already." He answered, sounding very annoyed.

"No, at least I don't think so...What is she doing here?"

"Obviously, she's there to take care of you." The wind whistled through the phone. A door slammed and the reception was clear. "She's doing that?"

"Yes." I rolled my eyes at him. "She's being downright annoying. Making me food and forcing pills into me."

"Good." He growled and the line went dead.

The screen flashed and then went black. Kaleb knew Delilah was here and he was being as cryptic as ever. Getting a straight answer from him would take a miracle. I leaned back against my pillows and flicked through the channels. *Friends* were playing. It would work. The characters were laughing and having a good time. Never mind. My mood couldn't handle the light carefree acting. The TV shut off with a blink.

"Delilah!" I called out. Footsteps jogging down the hall alerted me to her presence. The door creaked open and her head poked inside.

"Do you need something, your royal froginess?" She frowned at me.

"Now that you mention it. I left something in the living room."

"What is it? I can get it for you." She started to leave the room.

"No. I want to do it for myself."

She rolled her eyes at me and advanced the wheelchair next to the bed. "If you would leave this within arm's reach, you could get out of bed more often."

I glared at her.

"Or never mind. Sit there like the King of Sheba waiting on his peons to do things for him." There was a bite to her words. "You have to use the chair if you're going to get it yourself," she muttered.

She kicked the brakes on the wheels. Her soft hands brushed against my skin as she slipped her arms undermine. A prickle of something ran across my skin where she touched me. Her full lips were at my ear as she lifted me. With a groan, my bad leg swung off the bed. It tangled in the sheets. A soft rip sounded as the sheet caught. We tumbled down to the ground, missing the wheelchair. Her soft body was beneath me as I looked into her eyes. For a second, my thoughts were stuck eleven years ago when we were in this same position in the hayloft. Her eyelids closed as her lips parted. Her breath came out in shallow puffs against my skin. I leaned closer to her lips. I was a hair away when her eyes jerked open and widened.

"Kade Tanner Kisment, that was a dirty joke." She shoved me off and on to the floor. Her hair was wild about her face. A blush covered her cheeks and she tugged at her shirt to straighten it. "I should leave you there for that." There was a fire in her eyes that I hadn't seen since high school and with a jolt, I realized I missed it.

I reached out to her. "Come on, Dee. It was an accident. My leg caught in the sheet. I didn't mean that." Of course, I hadn't intended on almost kissing her, but caught up in the moment, I forgot where I was. I needed to keep the present and the past separate if she was going to be here long term. I sat up and tried to hoist myself up on the bed, but with my broken ribs, I didn't have the upper body strength to get my body where I wanted it. Pausing to catch my breath, my casted leg slid out from under me, and down I went. "Help me...please."

"I hope that you hurt." She signed and her face softened a bit. She walked behind me and grasped me up by my armpits. She was strong. Her muscles strained and she grunted as she lifted me into the chair. She bustled around, setting the feet rests, and padding the back of the chair. Her hand gently brushed my shoulder as she pushed the chair out of the bedroom.

"Believe me, I do hurt."

"So, what do you need?" A small smile pulled at the corners of her lips. She padded my shoulder again. Almost like she cared about me.

# Chapter 8 September 1st

## Delilah

Working with this man might be the end of me. I wasn't sure the stunt in his bedroom was on purpose or an accident, even when he claimed it was an accident. He leaned toward me and it seemed like he was going to kiss me. Even though a part of me was begging for him to kiss me, I couldn't have that. I needed to protect my heart from him. He hurt it once before and I wasn't going to do that again. I pushed his wheelchair down the hall towards the kitchen.

"Are you hungry or want to watch TV?" I asked.

He grunted in response. I wheeled him into the kitchen and put the fixings for sandwiches on the counter where he could reach them. My phone vibrated in my pocket. "I got to get this." Melanie's name lit up the screen. I walked out to the porch.

"Hey girl," Melanie screeched through the phone. "I heard a rumor. Is it true?"

"Depends what the rumor is?" I twisted a long strand of hair around my finger as I leaned against a post, waiting on her to continue as cows meandered passed in the field.

"I heard that a certain bull rider is in town." Her voice took on a sing-song sound.

"I heard that too," I said, with a sigh. *What was she getting at?*

"I also heard he has a new nurse." Melanie pressed on.

I wasn't going to give into her. Instead, I said, "Kaleb said he had a lot of nurses."

"Ha. I knew you knew things." She laughed. She was probably pointing at me through the phone. "How are you talking to Kaleb nowadays?"

"I ran into him in the grocery store." I pulled out some gum and popped it into my mouth. The peppermint flavor exploded on my tongue. Melanie was not going to let this one go.

"Come on, Delilah. Just tell me where you are. I went by the apartment to see you and your stuff is packed up."

"Fine," I rolled my eyes and snapped my gum. "I am at the Kisment ranch...Taking care of Kade." Silence came from the other side. "Melanie."

"Is that the smartest idea? Are you sure you can be in the same room as him?" I knew she was going to be worried. She found out about Kade and me a couple of months ago when Pete's cows got out. Kade was in town for the rodeo and at Pete's ranch when she briefly met him.

"Yes, we need this." I dropped my voice to a whisper. "It's going to help get the riding stable off the ground. You won't have to ask Pete or your parents to help us."

"But at what cost?" Her voice was soft

"I'll be fine." *That's what I kept telling myself.* "It was a long time ago." *Also, what I kept telling myself and maybe I will believe it one day.*

"I'm worried about you, and I don't want you to get hurt. If you ever need anything, give me a call. Love you."

"Love you too. Melanie. Don't worry it will be ok."

A click sounded in my ear and I slipped it back into my pocket. My gum snapped when a clatter came in from the kitchen. *Back to work, Delilah.* I went back inside.

"What are you doing?" I swung open the screen door to see Kade straining toward the coffee pot, from the wheelchair.

The coffee maker was pushed up against the back wall and three inches from his fingertips. The knife block had tipped over scattering knives over the counter, and a couple of pots and pans were on the floor. Kade had a sheepish grin on his face as he glanced over at me.

"Making coffee. Do you want any?" He gripped the edge of the counter and inched towards the coffee pot. "I'm having problems reaching the coffee machine."

"Just how were you going to put a filter in the pot?" I approached his side to stare at his clear blue eyes, for a moment.

Kade shrugged and snagged the pot with a long finger. "If you could pour the water, I will get the rest."

I filled the reservoir with fresh water as he scooped the coffee grounds into the filter, sprinkling cinnamon on top before handing me the filter. I seated it in the coffee maker before turning it on. I raised my eyebrows at him.

"I remembered you like a little cinnamon in your coffee." A smile pulled at the edges of his lips and his eyes crinkled.

After all these years and he remembered how I like my coffee! Then, he shrugged before settling further in the wheelchair and wheeling into the living room. "Bring the coffee when it is done." He called over his shoulder.

The demand grated on my nerves as I tried not to grind my teeth. He was always so arrogant. But he remembered how I drank my coffee, and I wondered what else he remembered. I shook my head at the thought. To buy some time, I cleaned the kitchen as the coffee brewed, the knives went back in the block, the pots and pans were put away, and the counters scrubbed. The coffee maker buzzed as the last bit of the black liquid dripped into the large glass pot. The smell of coffee and cinnamon permeated throughout the house.

"Delilah, are you coming with that coffee? I heard it beep." His voice demanded from the living room.

"Great. The annoying Kade was back," I muttered as I poured each of us a mug and made my way into the living room.

He'd settled himself in the middle of the room staring at the bull riding event on the TV. He leaned forward in his chair taking the mug from me, wrapping his hands around the mug, and glancing at me before going back to the bulls and cowboys. I sank into the overstuffed recliner in the corner to savor my hot mug for a minute.

A cowboy in black chaps mounted a large white bull. The cowboy nodded as the chute gate swung open. The bull burst from the chute, bucking, twisting, and snorting. The cowboy hung on until a buzzer rang. Kade slammed his fist into his armrest. A list of profanities came from his mouth. I looked over at him in surprise.

"There's a lady in the house." I tossed a throw pillow at him. He ducked, spilling his coffee over his lap.

"Hot! Hot! Hot!" He squirmed in his seat. I ran to get a towel from the kitchen and raced back to him. I dabbed at his lap to soak up the coffee.

"I am so sorry." I sputtered. I dabbed and rubbed at his lap some more.

"Um, Dee. Can you stop?" He cleared his throat and adjusted in the chair.

My eyes met his. Heat raced up my chest and cheeks when I realized where my hand was resting. I jerked it away, but he caught it between his. He drew me closer until his lips touched mine for the briefest moment before he drew away. My heart and mind were twisting and turning. What did it mean? Why did he do that? I stood there staring at him when Kaleb strolled into the house.

"The coffee smells wonderful." His words dropped off as he walked into the living room. "Look at what we have going on." He crossed his arms and leaned against the door frame.

"It was nothing." Kade slid his chair back.

"Yep, nothing going on." I stepped back and flipped my hair behind my shoulders. "Kade spilled his coffee and needed help."

"He does need help." He laughed and he went back into the kitchen.

"What was with all the swearing?" I whispered to Kade, but he just shook his head.

"Do you know who that was?" His voice dropped as he leaned toward me. "Jose Garcia just moved up into the number one spot now that I'm out of the race for the world champion title." The bitterness dripped from his lips as they turned into a snarl, his eyes grew black, and he withdrew into himself. "Take me back to my room." The hurt in his eyes broke my heart. *How did he end up this way?* I tried to keep my face neutral as I wheeled his chair to his room.

# Kade

JOSE GARCIA RODE HIS bull for a 94-point ride. A perfect ride was 100 but no one ever had a hundred-point ride. Any score over 90 points was good. It pushed him into the first spot, and I fell to the number two spot. I had been the number one rider in the country but with my accident, the other riders accumulated more points while I was out. The rider with the most points would lead the rankings heading into the Bull Riding Finals. It would be only a matter of time before another rider passed me up while I sat in bed watching them on TV. That should have been me. I should be the number one bull rider. But, no, I was stuck in my home with the one person I had ever loved taking care of me. At least, she was taking care of me today.

After wheeling me into my room, she helped me to bed, making sure the pillows were fluffed, and the wheelchair was placed within reach. She set a glass of water and a package of fruit pastries next to the bed on the nightstand before leaving the room.

Night fell and the house grew even more silent than normal. It was normally a quiet house with only me and Kaleb living here. He went to bed early so he could be up before dawn to start work on the ranch. My clock read midnight and the restlessness overcame me. I strained and lifted myself into the chair. Slowly, I wheeled myself out of my room and down the hall. A light came from the living room. I rolled to the doorway and stopped. Delilah sat in the corner of the couch with a lamp shining over her shoulder. It cast a halo of light onto her hair. I smiled as I thought about how angelic she looked. She hunched over a laptop and typed furiously, like a madwoman.

I cleared my throat, causing her to jump. The laptop fell towards the floor before she caught it and shut it with a snap. She uncurled her legs. She slid the blanket covering her down the couch.

"Kade, you surprised me." She placed a hand on her chest. "My heart is just racing." She placed the laptop next to her on the couch. She slowly stood, eyeing me.

"What are you doing here?" I narrowed my eyes at her. "Don't you have a fancy apartment in San Antonio to go to?"

She straightened her back and raised her chin a tab. "I'm working."

"Obviously...Can't you do that somewhere else?" I rolled my chair closer to her, backing her into a corner.

"No, I'm working here, in this house." She sighed and sunk back into the couch. "Kaleb wants me to sleep here."

"Why?" *Of all of Kaleb's ideas, this one was crazy.*

"To care for you." She cocked her head at me as her black hair fell over a shoulder. I wanted to reach out and stroke it. My hand raised of its own volition, before I realized what it was doing, I snatched it back to my lap.

"Wait, you are my nurse?" I narrowed my eyes at her as understanding dawned on me.

"Took you long enough." She retorted. She drew up her long legs and tucked them under her, pulling the blanket back over her lap. "Kaleb hired me to take care of you and as part of the arrangement I have to stay here." My brow furrowed as I looked at her. "I'm more than qualified to dote on your every whim. I can send you my resume` if you're concerned."

"No need." I rolled back towards the kitchen. "Are you hungry?"

"Are you cooking?" She unfolded herself from her seat.

"Only if you do everything for me. What do you want to make?" I tried to chuckle to break the awkwardness of the moment.

"Frozen pizza, ok?" She asked.

Delilah followed me into the kitchen. Her bare feet padded on the floor. She moved with the ease of being comfortable in her environment, getting the oven on and finding the pizza stone. After some time, the smells of bubbling sauce and cheese filled the air. She sat on the chair across the table from me.

"Do you want to play a game of cards?" She tapped her nails on the tabletop in a nervous gesture that she had back in high school.

"Sure. How about letting me make up a new game?" I winked at her, causing a faint blush to color her cheeks.

"I am not stripping." She rolled her eyes at me and snapped her gum before heading to the junk drawer. She reached into the drawer and pulled out a worn-out deck of cards. My siblings and I spent many hours playing with that deck, and it was missing a few cards.

"No, I was thinking war and whoever has the losing turn has to answer a question." I rolled my wheelchair closer to the table and leaned my elbows on it to look into her beautiful eyes.

"Fine, but if you ask something I don't want to answer, I am not going to." She shuffled the cards, cut the deck, and shuffled it again. She slid it across the worn wooden table. I cut the deck and she dealt the deck in half. The top cards were discarded. The first hand was laid down. She had a five of diamonds to beat my three of clubs.

"In all of your travels, where's your favorite place to travel to?" She snapped her gum.

"That's easy. The Chicago bull ride in January." A questioning look crossed her face. "I love the snow. I wish we got it down here more often." Next hand, I laid down a King of spades to Delilah's Jack of hearts. I grinned at her.

"Where did you go to college?"

"Western New York University." She slapped the next card down it was an Ace. I put down an Ace. We laid a couple of cards each and flipped the last one.

"I win!" I fist-pumped the air before scooping the cards into my pile. The cracked ribs shot pain through my side at the sudden movement. I grabbed my side and wheezed for a second. "Do you have any pets?"

"I have a betta fish. He's in Katie's room. His purple clashes with the pink of the room." She laughed a bit at that, her eyes brightening a bit.

On the next hand, Delilah won and asked, "are you really still driving that old truck parked outside?"

I nodded as I laid down the next round. Having won that hand, I asked. "How are you available to nurse me back to health?"

"I quit my job." She straightened the cards in front of her.

"Before or after I got hurt?" I held my breath hoping she did it for me. *Wow, where did that come from?*

She raised her eyebrows at me and shook her head. "Only one question." She laid down her next hand. I won again. I inhaled and steadied my hands. Time to go for broke.

"Do you ever think about me?"

She rocked back in the chair, balancing on two legs, and stared at me. I thought that she wasn't going to answer that one. She reached over her shoulder to twirl her hair around her finger. I leaned towards her and grasped at her hand. Her gaze held mine and the corners of her eyes softened.

"Yes," she whispered. "More than is healthy."

The timer buzzed for the pizza. She jerked her hands from mine and ran to get the pizza out of the oven. My mind whirled with her response. Did I hear her right? 'More than is healthy.'

Maybe I had a shot at her affections again. She brought the golden-brown cheese pizza over to the table. She set the pizza cutter down next to my hand.

"I'm starving," she said.

Tension settled between us that wasn't there a moment before.

# Chapter 9 September 8th

## Kade

The ringing of the rusty triangle stirred me from my dreams of Delilah. I hadn't dreamt of her in a long time. She was the one person I tried to block out of my life after that day. I let her down and broke her heart. I was a coward, and I spent the next part of my life running from that decision. I rubbed the sleep from my eyes and stared into the harsh light in my room. It wasn't morning anymore. The clock read 1:00 P.M. I groaned and shifted in the bed, pain radiated out from my ribs and leg as my head pounded to a beat of its own. I reached for the nightstand only to knock the open pill bottle to the floor. The pills skittered to all corners of the room with a clatter. Zip jumped up and tried to get them.

"Zip, no!" I lurched forward to grab his color before he left the bed. Pain shot up my side and darkened the edges of my vision. I wrapped my fingers into his collar and held on. My teeth clenched. I tried to stay conscious through the next wave of pain.

The door cracked open and Delilah entered the room. She surveyed me trying to hold onto my dog. Zip attempted another leap off the bed and a grimace crossed my face. She walked over to Zip and scooped the wiggly heeler up into her arms.

"I'll be right back. Let me take him outside." She crossed the floor, gracefully avoiding several of the small white pills littering the rug. She shouldered her way through the door and went down the hall.

"Everything alright?" Kaleb's voice echoed from the kitchen.

"Under control. I think Zip wanted some of Kade's pain meds." Her voice strained as she moved further away.

"Here, I'll take him from you." A chair scraped on the kitchen floor and Kaleb's spurs rang out with each step.

"Thanks, Kaleb."

*Was it me or did her voice sound a little brighter when she talked to him? Did she have something going on with Kaleb? Is that why she is here?* I straightened myself in the bed as her footsteps hurried back to my room.

"Morning, Kade. Or should I say, afternoon," she said briskly. "I can get those for you." She bent over and carefully picked up each stray pill. Her white T-shirt rode up on her lower back, revealing a tattoo that had horses and hearts on it.

"I didn't know you had a tramp stamp," I growled at her. She looked up sharply and glared. A look of hurt crossed her face.

"You don't know everything about me." She retorted before crawling further under the bed to reach a few more.

"Really? I know quite a bit." I crossed my arms, my jaw clenched as I thought about who else saw her tattoo. A shot of jealousy bolted through me. I didn't want anyone else to see her like that, and that thought surprised me.

She scooted from under the bed and sat back on her heels. She cocked her head as her black hair fell to the side. She pushed it out of the way before standing up.

"Like I know you and Kaleb have some sort of thing going on. I can see the way you look at him. You taking care of me is some sick joke to you, isn't it? 'Look at the poor, helpless Kade Kisment. He can't even get out of bed on his own.'" I glared at her. Her brown eyes went dark as the color left her skin. *I knew I was right.*

"You are a jerk." She twisted the cap on the bottle and threw it at me. It hit me in the forehead before I could catch it. She stomped towards the door, pausing over her shoulder. "You gave up every right to me the night you walked out on me...on us." The door slammed behind her. She stormed to the kitchen. Her steps pounded on the floor. I could feel the vibrations in my room. Kaleb's voice mixed with hers, but I couldn't make out what they were saying. Then, the screen door slammed, and the house was quiet for a minute. I swallowed the pain medication I needed dry as the water glass was empty. I leaned against the headboard and closed my eyes until the door creaked open and Kaleb blocked the doorway with his big frame.

"When she comes back you are going to apologize to her." He glowered at me.

"Everything I said was true."

"You wouldn't know the truth if it ran you over and gored you with its horns. Apologize when she comes back."

"Or what?" *What could he do to me?* I raised my chin to him.

"I am taking you to a rehab facility and leaving you there." He crossed his arms. "Kurt already suggested that if you run out Delilah."

"You wouldn't," I said, glaring right back at him. I hated that Kurt threw his money around to get people to do what he wanted.

"Don't make me do it." He was gone with the door shut firmly behind him.

*Apologize to Delilah? Kaleb's insistence all but proved that they had a thing going on. They were probably cuddling on the couch and having a good laugh at my expense.* I punched my pillow and allowed sleep to replace the anger I had inside, at least for a while.

A couple of hours later, I couldn't get comfortable. My back and butt hurt. My head ached and my mouth parched. My tongue was heavy in my mouth. The water glass next to the bed was empty, and my wheelchair sat across the room. There was no way I could hobble, hop, or crawl that distance. Plus, once I got there, I wouldn't be able to lift myself into the chair. A sigh of frustration left my lips.

"Kaleb!" I called. No response. No steps came. No swearing at me that he will be right there.

"Delilah!" No response to that one either. The house was stiller than normal. I picked up my phone and called Kaleb.

"What." He answered.

"I need help," I said.

"Call Delilah or figure it out." The line went dead with a buzz.

I scrolled through my phone. I didn't have her on my contact list. I dialed the only number I remembered of hers. It went straight to voice mail, and it wasn't a helpful voicemail as it was one that repeated the numbers back to me. I hung up. My only other option was to try Damien, Delilah's brother, and someone who had been one of my closest friends growing up. It was the middle of the afternoon, but I was starting to become desperate. Damien's phone rang a couple of times before he answered it.

"Hi Damien, it's Kade." We'd been friends for a long time. Hopefully, he'd help me. I crossed my fingers.

"Hey, buddy. How are you? Long time no see," he said hesitantly.

"Could be better. Could be worse." I laughed bitterly. "I'm home for a while with an injury."

"I heard. The rumor mill has been busy."

"Anything good?" I asked, maybe small talk will soften him up.

There was a silence from him. Damien wasn't a talkative guy, but he was straightforward. There was something he didn't want to share. "Nah, just all about you. Would you be up to going out some night? Pete needs a real bachelor party with the guys."

"Sure. I can wheel it. I had forgotten that Pete was engaged."

"He wasted no time. The gal is Melanie. You remember? She started the dress shop back up... A real sweetheart." The unsaid hung in the air. If I'd paid attention to the people that mattered to me, I'd remember.

"I think I met her last time I was home." She must have been the pretty brunette hanging around Pete. Good for him. "I was calling to get Dee's number."

Another silence.

"Do you want to talk to her?" His voice dropped and sent shivers up my spine.

"That's why I called you."

"Hang on." It sounded like he put the phone down. "Dee, Kade is on the phone for you." He shouted. Her response was muffled. Damien laughed. "Sorry bro, she says you can kiss her behind. That you are a self-centered jerk and unequivocal something that I am not going to repeat with my mother standing here."

I sighed, that was so Delilah. "Fine, can you tell her I am sorry and... that I need her."

A very pregnant silence followed, and it seemed to go on forever.

"What are you sorry for and why do you need her?" Damien was quiet, and the words rumbled in the air. "She is my baby sister."

The protectiveness of his little sister came through the line loud and clear.

"Tell her I am sorry for what I said to her today and I need her help to get out of bed."

Damien gave a short sharp laugh at that. "I'll tell her but that is all." The line went dead.

*What is with people hanging up on me today?* I tried to plump the pillows. I scooted one down on the mattress to sit on. It helped the numb sensation in my lower extremities. I flicked the TV on to distract myself from the discomfort I was in.

On the eighth episode of *Friends*, the screen door banged. Finally, my salvation is here. Heavy footsteps stomped to my room and the door flung open like it was in a hurricane.

"Kade Tanner Kisment, you are the slime on a toad's belly for calling my brother." She stomped toward the bed. She never looked madder or hotter. Her cheeks were flushed a rosy pink. Her shiny black hair floated around her face and down her shoulders. Her T-shirt rode up her flat abdomen as she flailed her arms around her face so much I got lost in her looks.

"Are you even listening to me?" She shouted.

I mentally shook myself. "Huh?"

"You called my brother to have me come over." She poked me in the chest with each word, hard.

"Ouch." I rubbed at the spot. "I am sorry. I was mean but I need your help. Please."

Her look softened a bit, and her arms went back to her side. She stopped for a second and then grabbed the wheelchair from the corner.

"You've never apologized to me before. For anything." She said so quietly I almost didn't catch it. *She was right I never apologize for anything. Boy, did I have a lot to be sorry for with Delilah*. She brought the chair closer and helped me in it. She pushed me out of the room into the hallway.

"Where to next, your highness?" She did an elaborate curtsy and gestured around the house. I smiled at her and got an almost genuine smile in response.

## Delilah

KADE WAS INFURIATING. When he walked out on me eleven years ago, he never looked back. I had called him and left him messages. No answer. But I had to get on with my life. I would have never thought I'd find myself pushing his wheelchair around the house. He wanted to go sit outside on the porch, so I wheeled him out the door.

"Where are you going?" He called over his shoulder as I set the brake and headed back into the house.

"To get some pillows or something. I bet your backside is sore." I pushed through the door. "You don't have any padding back there," I muttered as I swept up some pillows and a comforter from the couch to add to the swing. "Here you go." The swing swayed gently in the breeze as I arranged the pillows and blanket to pad the wooden swing. "You can sit here with your leg propped up."

Kade rolled close to the swing. As he reached out towards me, our hands touched, electric sparks tingled up my arm as I helped him into the swing. The old flame of desire flared at his touch. It reminded me of how gentle and caring he was when we were a couple. He loved me and showed it all the time. I tamped down the old feelings and focused on being a nurse. The rust chains creaked as he sat down. His sky-blue eyes met mine and my heart pounded.

I broke the contact, lifting his right leg onto another pillow. "Here's some ice." I packed it around the leg. I wiped my hands on my pants. He caught my hands in his and rubbed his thumb over the back of mine. A small smile pulled at the corners of his mouth. Unsaid thoughts swirled in his eyes and drew me in. *Was there still something between us? Could there be something between us? Or is there too much hurt?* I mentally shook myself back to my job, trying to not let my heart fall for Kade all over again.

"Why don't you get some sweet tea and sit with me?" He gave me big puppy dog eyes and motioned to the chair next to him. *Could I sit next to him? Can I protect my heart?* The wariness must have shown on my face. "Come on, Dee. I am sorry about this afternoon. I promise I will be nice."

I sighed and pulled my hair back into a ponytail as I headed back into the kitchen. "Fine. I'll get us some cookies and sweet tea."

I handed him a glass of sweet tea and a package of sandwich cookies before plopping into the rocking chair next to him. I threaded my fingers together and placed them behind my head. The sun beat down on us. The cows mooed as they inched their way across the pasture next to the house, looking for blades of grass. The wind blew tiny gusts across the flat pasture, stirring up small twists of dust. I rocked back and forth. I tried to keep my thoughts from the man sipping sweet tea and munching on cookies.

"So, you and Kaleb are an item?" His quiet voice filled the awkward silence between us.

"No." I scoffed. His expression was unreadable. "Why?"

"Isn't Kaleb a nice guy? Or is he not your type?" He swirled the tea around in his glass. The ice cubes clunked together.

I cut my eyes to him. *What was he getting at? Did I have feelings for Kaleb? Seriously, he was asking me that? I don't even know what to say to that.* "He's a nice guy and I know a lot of girls in town find him attractive." I narrowed my eyes at him and shrugged.

"You don't like him?" He set his cookies down and leaned forward.

"Seriously, Kade. He's like an older brother I don't need. Damien is enough for one girl." I studied him as he fidgeted on the swing. "Why? Are you jealous?" I tried not to smirk. *That's it. Kade Kisment was jealous of me and his older brother. Ha, that was funny.*

"I can't figure out why Kaleb has you helping me." He shook his head but still did not meet my eyes.

"You ran away all the other in-home nurses and he figured I could stick with it." I kicked off my shoes and drew circles in the air with my toes. The silence stretched on.

"He's paying you?" Kade's eyelids raised and his hand stopped midway to his mouth.

I turned to look at him and nodded.

"But don't you have a job." His brow wrinkled as if this was a hard concept.

"I quit my job. I told you that. And he's paying." I shrugged and reached over to steal a cookie.

"Are you only here for money?" He looked hurt and those big blue eyes widened into an incredibly sad puppy dog look.

"Really, Kade? I've avoided you and your whole family for the last eleven years. Do you think I would do this out of the goodness of my heart without getting paid?" I scoffed. I rocked back in the chair.

"No, I guess not." He sucked down the rest of the sweet tea. "I kind've wished you did it just to be with me."

It was so soft that I almost didn't hear it. *I guess I am going to ignore that comment.* I rocked back and forth. The awkwardness got thick and I didn't know what to say to that.

"I'm going to get dinner ready. Don't eat all the cookies." I grabbed my shoes and went inside.

# Kade

DELILAH COULD ALWAYS see through me. I should've known she was going to guess about my feelings for her and Kaleb. The two of them together got my heart pounding and I wanted to smash something. I wished I had let it alone. Whenever I was with her, I had to remind myself that we were not together, and it was my fault as was most of what went wrong in my life. I didn't deserve to have a woman like her. The banging in the kitchen interrupted my ruminations. Water ran in the sink as a knife thudded dully against the wood cutting board.

My cell phone rang in my pocket as a name flashed across the screen that I had not seen in a while. I swiped to answer it.

"Hello?" Trepidation clutched in my chest.

"Hey, Kade. It's Veronica." Her high-pitched voice made me cringe.

"How's it going, Veronica?" At that, all the noise in the kitchen stopped. "Is everything ok?" For a second, I thought about how I had forgotten all about her and her daughter since I got hurt. Guilt consumed me. If something were wrong, I'd never been able to forgive myself. Veronica's husband, Ben, was my traveling partner. When he died, I stepped in to make sure that they were taken care of.

"Yes. We're getting by. I heard about your accident and was calling to see if there is anything I can do?" Her voice was sweet and almost pleading.

I sighed with relief that she was okay. "It was about a month ago," I said as I ran my fingers through my hair.

She laughed nervously. "I'm a little out of the loop with Ben gone and all. I don't follow the bull riding circuit like I used to." She had a hint of sadness in her voice.

"No, it's ok. I'm just recovering at home."

"Do you need someone to care for you? Do you need any help? You've helped us so much; I want to return the favor." She was stumbling over her words as she hurried to get them out.

"Nah, I'm good. My brothers have it handled." I bit into the second to last cookie. Delilah's shadow crept out under the screen door.

"Ok. Just let me know if you need any help." She paused for a second. "Oh, Kade, you don't have to send a check this month."

"Are you sure?" I sat up and stopped chewing. I handled her finances and every month I sent her a check for living expenses. Veronica was a sweetheart, but Ben said she wasn't good with budgeting. "Everything's alright?" Nerves ran through me if something had happened to them, I'd never forgiven myself.

"Yep." Her voice hit a high note and squeaked. "All's good. We have a bunch of leftover from last month. We can make it work for a bit."

"Alright. Let me know if you need more. Bye, Veronica."

"Bye, Kade."

I sighed and stretched my arms over my head, flinching as I forgot about the pain in my ribs. I set my phone down and closed my eyes, leaning my head against the cold chain. A shadow fell on my face as someone blocked out the sun.

"You're unbelievable." Delilah crossed her arms and glared at me. "You accused me of being something to Kaleb and you have a girl. What do you want of me? Just to make myself a nun?"

I shrugged. I didn't want to explain the phone call or myself to her. She stormed back into the house, slamming the door. I closed my eyes and tried not to worry about Delilah or Veronica or any of their problems.

The wind blew softly, and the cows mooed close by. A horse trotted into the yard with its metal shoes clanging against the small gravel. The horse snorted and blew as the saddle creaked. Then, heavy boots clopped up the porch steps. Kaleb reached and took the last cookie from the plate that Delilah had made for me.

"It's good to see you out of the house." He propped one foot up on the edge of a chair and leaned towards me. "Feeling better?" I nodded at him. A loud crash came from the kitchen, causing us both to turn. "She's still mad?"

"Yep, like a hornet."

Kaleb chuckled and shoved the whole cookie in his mouth. "You do have that effect on her. I'll go check it out." He strode confidently towards the kitchen. He had a swagger to his stride that I haven't seen in a while. Delilah might not have feelings for him, but he looked excited to confront her in all her rage. The screen door slammed behind him, and I strained to make out what they were saying, but all I heard was mumbling. A few minutes went by before Delilah came out of the kitchen. She swept by me without even a glance, gathered the reins of the horse, and swung on to his back. She clucked to him, and off they trotted down the lane and out of sight. Her black hair floating behind her contrasting with the grey horse.

"What do you want for dinner?" Kaleb leaned against the door. "Delilah burnt the noodles for the mac and cheese."

"Sandwiches are fine. Where's she going?"

Kaleb shrugged. "She just needs to ride it out. I told her to take the rest of the day off." He went back into the kitchen. I watched the horse and rider get smaller on the horizon. My feelings for her both surprised and confused me. What was I going to do?

# Chapter 10 September 9th

## Delilah

I poured myself a cup of coffee when Kaleb entered the kitchen. He filled his thermos with the rest of the pot of the black gold before turning his attention to me.

"I need you to take Kade to his doctor's appointment this morning." He grabbed a banana from the counter and peeled it. "The veterinarian is coming today to pregnancy check the spring calving cows. I don't want to reschedule. He has a month-long wait period."

"Wow. He needs to hire someone if he is that busy."

"He said he hired a new veterinarian. But he won't start until this spring." He shoved the banana in his mouth.

"I can take Kade. It's a recheck?" *What else could I say? I don't want to be in the same small space as him. Stuck there for hours and hours. Think of the money, Delilah.* I told myself. I put on a grin and nodded.

"Yes, and probably he'll get x-rays and a new cast. Here's the appointment card. See you tonight." He slapped his cowboy hat on his head and strode out.

The business card held the address of Kade's surgeon, Dr. Greg Glanders, and the time of the appointment. Great, Dr. Glanders my ex-boyfriend. Maybe, I'd get lucky and another surgeon would be seeing his appointments. I could only hope. It was in two hours.

I approached Kade's bedroom and silently swung the door open. He fell asleep only a couple of hours earlier. Part of my job was to monitor his sleeping and medications overnight. I usually check on him every couple of hours. Last night, his pain had been excruciating and he spent most of the night tossing and turning. I tiptoed across the room. The floor creaked a bit. I stopped on the rug and held my breath.

"Delilah, I know you're there." He mumbled into the pillow, not picking up his head to look at me. "What do you want?"

"You have a doctor's appointment in a couple of hours. We need to leave in forty-five minutes."

He groaned and pulled the blankets over his head. I slid open the curtains to let the morning light into the room. He groaned again and rolled towards the wall.

"Can't it be rescheduled?"

"No, you have a good surgeon and he probably won't have any openings for at least a week." I moved his chair closer to the bed. "Besides, you need different pain medications. You haven't slept well for the last couple of nights." I hadn't slept either. Thinking about the man across the hall made me toss and turn. Kade finally rolled back over and scooted to the edge of the bed.

"Alright, let's do this." A sarcastic smile pulled at one side of his lips.

The waiting room of the hospital was crowded. Kade wheeled his wheelchair to a corner of the waiting room so I snagged a wooden chair and dragged it over next to him. We stared out the glass window, watching the traffic below, not talking to each other. He folded his arms across his chest as a large sigh escaped his lips. I turned in my chair to watch him. I forgot how much I liked just to sit next to him as butterflies danced in my stomach.

"Do you want to talk about yesterday?" He asked. His blue eyes searched my face. I blushed and fidgeted with my keys.

"Not really." I was embarrassed about how I acted. I didn't know why I was jealous of another woman in Kade's life, and I didn't want to examine it that closely. Silence settled between us as we both were lost in our thoughts.

"Do you remember the first time we met?" His voice was soft and hard to hear over the hum of the room.

I shook my head. "I thought you were always in my life."

A deep chuckle resonated from his chest. "Damien invited me over to play Legos after school, and your family had just moved to Sunnydale." A smile touched his lips. "You wanted to play with us. But Damien said no girls. Then you burst into his room wearing his shirt and shorts." He chuckled. "You said that you are now a boy. You were so cute." His blue eyes twinkled at me with a look I hadn't seen in years.

"I don't remember that," I murmured. I reached for his hand. My hand was hairs away from his when warning bells went off in my mind. *What was I doing? This is the same man that broke my heart in two.* A nurse walked into the room and called out Kade's name. He spun his chair around and wheeled it after her as I hurried to keep up.

Kade sat on the paper-covered bench in his shorts. The nurse had cut off the cast on his right leg and took him for radiographs. She brought him back and left us to wait for the doctor to look at the images. He scrolled on his phone as I paged through a magazine when a sharp knock sounded on the door. The doctor came in pushing a cart. My heart skipped a beat. He was tall, dark, and handsome. My skin heated as soon as I recognized him: Dr. Greg Glanders, orthopedic surgeon extraordinaire and my latest ex-boyfriend. I scooted closer to the door. Kade gave me a weird look before turning his attention back to the doctor.

"Good afternoon, Kade. Here for your four-week recheck, I see. How have you been feeling?" He punched buttons on his keyboard.

"Just fine," Kade muttered.

"How's the breathing?" He ran his fingers along Kade's ribs. Kade's face turned a little green. "It's only been four weeks, so you still have some time to heal, but your radiographs look good. They are healing nicely." The doctor moved down to palpate Kade's leg. "Any concerns?"

Kade shook his head.

*Of course, he would deny it!* Before I knew what was happening, my mouth opened. "Actually, Doctor," The doctor turned to face me. "Kade's been having a hard time sleeping from all the pain."

A smile lit up the doctor's face. "Why, Delilah Allen! I didn't see you there." I extended my hand to shake his. Instead, he wrapped me into a hug, that lasted a bit too long. I wiggled out of his grasp, catching Kade's glance. "Kade, you have the best nurse in the ER taking care of you." Heat rose up my cheeks as I looked at my shoes. "Of course, we can get something to help him sleep." He went back to examining Kade who raised his eyebrows at me.

"Here's the prescription." He handed a sheet to Kade and then turned to me. "Delilah, would you like to get some lunch sometime?" I blushed again as Kade cut his gaze to me. His blue eyes blazed.

I opened my mouth to respond when Kade cut in. "Delilah, I think it is time to go home."

I shot Kade a dark look. "Greg, I would love to get lunch sometime. My number is the same."

Kade scowled at me while I smiled brightly at him. Greg looked between us with confusion on his face.

## Kade

I CLENCHED MY FISTS as Dr. Glanders flirted with Delilah. She blushed a lovely pink color at his attention. She brushed her hair back with the back of her hand and fluttered her eyelashes at him. *Did she just do that?* My eyes narrowed as he laid his hand on her shoulder. Her laugh was high and fake when a knock sounded at the door. The nurse stuck her head in.

"Dr. Glanders, do you want Kade to be back in a cast?" She carried boxes under her arm. The door swung closed behind her. Dr. Glanders drew his attention away from Delilah.

"Yes." He glanced back at Delilah. "I'll call you later."

"That would be great." She looked down at her shoes and twirled a loose strand of hair. With that, he strode out of the room. The nurse wrapped my leg and rolled on the casting material. She put pressure on my ankle to bend it and the casting material grew hot. When I tried not to wince, Delilah stepped over and reached for my hand as I raised an eyebrow at her.

"What was that about?" I slid my hand out of her grasp to the edge of the exam table and gripped it.

"Oh, nothing," she mumbled with more blushing.

The nurse snorted. Then, she glanced up apologetically. "Dr. Glanders still has the hots for you, Delilah." She wrapped another couple of rounds of casting around my calf. "Rumor has it he hasn't dated anyone since you broke it off with him." She folded the cotton wrap down and ran the cast material under the upper edge. Delilah sat down in the chair and crossed her arms. The nurse looked over her and sighed. "But it's not any of my business." She cleaned up her materials and ran her hands down the length of the cast once more. "That should do it. You'll need another appointment in two weeks for more radiographs and another cast." Then, she quickly left the room.

I scooted myself into my wheelchair and rolled toward the door. "I'm starving. Let's get lunch." Delilah followed behind me as I checked out.

Maria's Pasta Bar was packed with people even when it was not lunchtime. Simmering marinara and freshly baked garlic bread assaulted my senses when we entered the packed building. The hostess seated us in a corner booth and took our drink orders.

"I haven't been here in ages." Delilah grabbed a menu and scanned it for the specials. "I think the last time I was here was the night of my prom." She blushed again and quickly hid behind the menu.

"That was a great night." I chuckled. "You ordered the spaghetti with the giant meatball. Do you remember that?"

"Kade, how could you bring up one of the most embarrassing moments of my high school career?" She blew her straw wrapper at me. I caught it before it bounced off my nose.

"It is one of my fondest memories of us." I leaned forward and grabbed her hands before she snatched them back. "You tried to eat that meatball on a fork. When you bit into it, it fell off and rolled down the front of your white dress."

"My mom was so mad at us. You had to rush me home to put on the dress I wore to your prom the year before."

"That green dress. It was beautiful on you." Sighing, my eyes flashed.

I was nineteen years old again and I was taking Delilah to her senior prom. When she walked down the stairs at her mother's house, the world stopped. That green dress. It was made for her and I loved it when she wore it the year before for my senior prom. A look of nostalgia crossed Delilah's face as if she were also remembering that night. *Was there something there? Something that missed how we used to be?* Her brown eyes got wider, and she leaned closer to me. Her lips parted when a throat clearing jerked us back to reality.

"Would you like to order?" The waitress asked sweetly.

Delilah dropped my hand and returned to the menu. "I would like the spaghetti and giant meatball." She winked over at me as I tried not to laugh.

"I will have the chicken alfredo." The waitress spun on her heel back to the kitchen, leaving Delilah to sip from her water.

"So, you and Dr. Glanders?" I leaned back to prop my leg up on the seat as Delilah choked on her water.

"Yep," She flicked a couple of drops of water at me. "We dated for a bit. Nothing serious."

"That's too bad. He looked at you like you were the last woman on earth."

"I don't need a man like that in my life." She shrugged. "He needed to be needed and it caused a lot of tension. Not to mention he was boring." She rolled her eyes up to look at the ceiling.

"Are you going to go to lunch with him?" I realized I had twisted my paper napkin into a small knot.

"Maybe." She leaned on the table. "Or maybe not." Her eyes glinted, her hair falling over her shoulders. "Would that bother you?"

*I wasn't going to admit it to her, but it bothered me greatly.* I sipped my sweet tea, surprised at my reaction to her question. She leaned closer still. Mischief danced in her eyes.

"Maybe." I leaned closer to her. "Maybe it does or maybe it doesn't."

I was so close I could see the gold specks in her irises, the ones that I had forgotten were there. Her hair swished forward, and the lavender scent of her shampoo wafted towards me. It reminded me of another time where I was close enough to see the gold specks in her eyes and the scent of lavender surrounded us. That night had been magical but had changed everything between us. Our first time together. Her hair splayed out around us and nothing but being together mattered to us.

I pulled back from her. I couldn't do this. I couldn't lead her into believing that I could be there for her. I wasn't strong enough. Walking away from her had been easier than staying with her. I knew I broke her heart, but I couldn't make myself stay for her. I was too weak to be her stronghold. I gulped the sweet tea.

"You and the doc would make a nice couple." I regretted the words as soon as they came out of my mouth. Her face fell. Her eyes narrowed and glistened. She tossed her hair over her shoulder.

"Excuse me, I need to visit the ladies' room." She slid out of our booth just as the waitress brought our food. "That was mean, Kade." She stormed to the back of the store.

I slumped in my seat. Pain spiked from my ribs at the sudden movement. I popped a couple of pills. It was for the best. She deserved someone to be there for her. I failed her once and I was afraid it would happen again. I didn't know if I could be the man she deserved.

## Delilah

THE WATER RAN IN THE sink, swirling around the drain. I stared at my reflection in the mirror. I'd escaped just in time before the tears started to fall. My mascara lined my lower lids and dripped down my cheek. I took a paper towel and dabbed at my eyes until the black was on the towel and not on my skin. I pinched my cheeks the way my grandmother used to do when I was little. She would dry my tears and then pinch my cheeks, saying it brought life back into them. I pushed my hair back into a low ponytail and straightened my shoulders.

"You can do this, Delilah." I coached myself in the mirror. "He's a stupid, obnoxious boy. You can do this. Think of the children." The children needed me to complete this assignment. The money would also feed the horses through the winter. People and horses were depending on me. I glared at myself again and turned to head back to the table.

Kade was on the phone with someone who was making him laugh. I stopped dead in my tracks realizing that it was my phone he was talking on. I cautiously approached the booth.

"Hang on. Here she is." He handed the phone over to me, smirking. "It's your friend Melanie."

"Hey, Melanie," I said cautiously.

"Delilah, I have some good news for you!"

"Lay it on me. I could use something good." Kade's eyebrows rose at this.

"I talked to Mr. Giffery's lawyer today," she paused and held her breath. The silence stretched for several minutes.

"Come on. You're killing me here! What did he say?" I bounced in my seat.

"There might be a chance that we could rent the stables and a few acres for a couple of months. His children are going to sell the property, but he anticipates it is going to take a long time to sell that much land."

"Oh, but that is only a temporary solution." At my words, Kade stopped eating and watched me. I fidgeted in my seat.

"I know, and I don't know how long we can keep the horses at Lindsay's place. They don't have enough hay to feed your crew for the winter. Mr. Giffery's place could buy us months or years... How have things been going on your end?"

"Alright. I have all the paperwork filled out for the permits once we have a sure place to be." Kade's eyes bored into me and I ignored him.

"Hang in there, girl. We will find something."

"I know. It'll get better in a few months." I smiled a bit as I thought about how far Kaleb's money would go to help us. It would secure a loan or even be a down payment on a place. I sighed as we hung up. I placed my phone face down on the table.

"What's going on?" Kade leaned his elbows on the table.

"Um...Melanie and I are trying to start a business." I don't know why I didn't tell him about our plans. It didn't feel like the right time. I wanted to keep this to myself, at least for right now.

"Is there anything I could help with?" The question startled me. Kade was good with horses, but children? I doubt he would know anything about them.

"No, I'm good." I shook my head, and he shrugged.

My steaming pile of spaghetti sat in front of me. I stabbed the meatball with my fork. It flew off the table and hit Kade in the chest. A large splotch of red stood out in the middle of his white T-shirt. His mouth dropped open into an O. A laugh burst out from me as he dabbed at his shirt.

"I think that is payback for the Greg comment." I laughed so hard tears streamed down my face. I clutched my side to keep upright. Kade stared at me before he started to laugh before pain crossed his face.

"My ribs hurt too much to laugh." He breathed out. "I did deserve that."

"I think I should stay away from the meatballs."

I missed hanging out and laughing with Kade. It brought back warm feelings of us spending hours at this restaurant talking and hanging out. A warmness spread throughout my body. Occasionally, I caught glimpses of the person I knew all those years ago. Maybe, he was still there. I mentally shook myself. I don't need a man in my life. I smiled at him when he grinned at me and winked. My heart broke into a thousand small pieces before I could stop it.

# Chapter 11 October 3rd

## Delilah

The three of us fell into a routine. It was almost like being back in high school when I was dating Kade and part of the Kisment family. Kaleb had breakfast going when I got up. He read the paper as I made the coffee because Kaleb's coffee was awful. He left for his day on the ranch and I went to check on Kade. He was either up watching the tiny TV on his dresser or scrolling through his phone. Or if he had a rough night with the pain, he might still be sleeping. This morning was no different. The last few nights were good as his ribs finally started to knit together. He could lay down to sleep instead of sitting up. He also was able to use his crutches for short distances. I swung open the door, carrying a tray of scrambled eggs and salsa. Kade was curled over on his side, squinting at his phone.

"Hey, Kade, what are you looking at?" I set the tray down and counted out the medications he needed to take with his food.

"The videos of the bull ride last night. But they are so small on my phone, it's hard to watch the guys ride." He glared at his phone before sitting up. "The eggs smell good."

"Kaleb made them," I said, earning me a brilliant smile from him in the morning as I wasn't a good cook. "Who won?" With that simple question, his smile turned upside down.

"Jose Garcia... again. He's been winning everything since I'm out of the picture." He stabbed his eggs harshly sending bits and pieces flying throughout the air. "What I wouldn't give to wipe that smug smile off of his face." He shoveled his eggs into his mouth like a starving man.

"When's the next competition?" I picked up power bar wrappers and sports drink bottles from his nightly snack. Then, opened the drapes.

"Tonight." Kade squinted at me in the sunlight. The doorbell peeled throughout the house causing Zip to leap off the bed, barking in the direction of the front door. "Are you expecting anyone?"

"No, it's not even seven AM... I'll go see who it is," I said as I made my way to the front of the house.

A shadow in the shape of a woman darkened the window in the screen door. I swung it open to see a woman with bright red hair standing with her finger raised to ring the bell, again. She had a large suitcase next to her with giant flamingoes parading around. Her red lips opened and closed into a large O. She was beautifully dressed in a flowing western dress with a silver and turquoise belt wrapping around her hips. Her eyes fell to my worn-out blue jeans and faded T-shirt. I tucked a hair behind my ear, trying not to feel like a slob.

"Oh, darling." She extended a well-manicured hand towards me. "I'm Veronica." Her hand was limp in mine. "I came to help Kade get better."

"Kade?" I asked, my brain not catching up on what was going on.

"Yes, darling. He lives here." She gave me a strange look and flounced by me into the house. She wheeled her suitcase into the kitchen and looked around. "Well, where is he?"

"Hang on, I'll go tell him."

I shook my head as I made my way down the hallway. I opened the door and stuck my head in. Kade was sitting in the middle of the bed, trying to get his pants over the bulky cast on his leg.

"Let me help you." Sighing, I marched over to him and yanked the jeans off his skinny legs. I adverted my eyes from what was above his knees. "There's no way these jeans are going to fit over this cast." I went through his dresser drawers and pulled out a pair of basketball shorts. "Here, wear these."

I tossed them at him. He caught them with one hand and winked at me.

"Who was at the door?" He slid into his shorts.

"She said her name was Veronica." I leaned against the wall and crossed my arms. A smile split his face before confusion clouded his eyes. "I take it you know her."

"Yes, I told her not to come."

"Is she an old girlfriend? Or a current girlfriend?" I tried to keep my tone light, but my voice cracked.

He chuckled and shook his head. "Not really." He reached for his crutches and left the room.

I had sunk on his bed. *What did that mean? Who was this person to him? Why had he not said anything? Why did I care?* That thought concerned me more than the woman in the kitchen. Maybe, I wasn't as impartial to him as I led myself to believe. Fury at myself and my unwanted feelings curled in my belly. I clutched the bedsheets in my fists and gritted my teeth. From the kitchen, happy screams in response to Kade's deep voice. I whipped the sheets from the bed and threw them into the pile at the door. "That man." It was going to be a long week for me. I sighed as I gathered up the sheets and stomped to the laundry room. The door slammed shut behind me

# Kade

WHEN A DOOR SLAMMED further within the house, I cringed. That was Delilah. My gaze fell to the woman draped around my neck. I guess she was pretty, but I'd never thought of her in that way. Many of the other bull riders drooled over her when she was around, but Ben, my traveling partner and Veronica's husband, always kept them away. He had been my closest friend on the circuit. A couple of years ago, he had an accident like mine, but he didn't make it. I made a promise to him on his death bed to watch out for Veronica and their little girl. I was caring for them ever since. I pried her fingers from around my neck and steered her towards the living room.

"Would you like something to drink? Tea, coffee, something stronger?" I asked.

Her big eyes slid down me from my cast to my crutches to my panting breath. Nodding, she brushed her fingers along my cheekbone, fluttering her eyelashes.

"We can sit in here and catch up." I motioned to the living room and hopped my way to the doorway.

"That sounds fantastic." She smiled brightly at me and sunk into the couch cushions. "Come sit next to me." She patted the cushion next to her and fluttered her eyelashes.

"Um, I'll get drinks first."

What was going on? Veronica had never acted like this before. There were no sparks or connection between us. The eyelashes, really. A sinking realization settled in my stomach. She had more than friendly feelings toward me. Why else would she be here? None of my other friends came to visit. Not that I blamed them. I had been a horrible friend to everyone from Sunnydale. I poured water into the coffee pot and pressed start. It gurgled and bubbled to life. Within a few minutes, it was filling the carafe` below. As most of the mugs were mismatched, different shapes, and chipped, I reached for the largest clean one to pour the coffee in it.

"What exactly do you think you are doing, Kade Tanner Kisment?" The voice startled me that I spilled some coffee on the counter. I wiped at it with my sleeve.

"Getting coffee for the guest."

"Obviously, but how do you intend to carry it without spilling?" Delilah stood in the doorway with her arms crossed and feet spread. Anger rolled off her towards me.

"I can manage." I chuckled inwardly. Delilah was jealous. It looked good on her.

One dark eyebrow arched upward as she watched me. I grabbed the mug with my good hand and held on to the crutch. I pivoted in place. My balance swung forward and backward, and the coffee lurched in the cup like it was on a ship. She smirked at me. I tried again, but I could not get myself to move forward. "Dee, please help me." I pouted and gave her big sad eyes. "I can't figure this out."

"It's not meant to be figured out. It can't be done without spilling or you falling," she said as she took the mug from me. She poured two more mugs and found a large cutting board that she improvised into service as a tray. "Let's go entertain your guest." She rolled her eyes when she thought I wasn't looking.

Veronica sat on the couch flipping through a cattle producer's magazine. Her stilettoes rested on the coffee table. Delilah snorted and then coughed behind me. Veronica glanced up at the noise.

"Kade, sit next to me." She purred as she moved over, patting the seat next to her.

"If it's all the same to you, the recliner is more comfortable for my leg." I hopped over to the overstuffed recliner in the corner. Delilah put down the tray, handing the largest mug to Veronica, and then she came over to help me get my leg elevated on a pillow.

"I'll be right back with some ice." She whispered in my ear. Her soft breath caused a shiver to go down my spine. Then, she was gone before I could respond. Veronica cleared her voice, drawing my attention over to her.

"Your maid is very pretty." She stirred sugar into her coffee. I shot her a look, but she avoided my eyes, concentrating on her coffee.

"She's not a maid. She's a good friend of mine who also happens to be a nurse." I reclined the chair back. "Her name is Delilah." My gaze held steady on her. She blushed and added more cream to her coffee. Delilah came back into the room carrying an arm full of reusable ice packs. She packed them around my leg before taking the chair in the opposite corner with her coffee.

"Veronica, where are you from? Kade has never mentioned you." Delilah smiled sweetly before sipping her drink.

I sighed. *Oh man, the claws were out.*

"I'm from Amarillo. Kade and I have been friends for an exceedingly long time." She handed the sugar to Delilah. "I haven't heard of you, either... Now that you mention it."

*Should I leave the room? Should I feign sleep?* The tension in the room increased exponentially as each woman sized the other up. I cleared my throat, trying to interrupt the conversation. Both women looked at me. *Oh no, I hadn't thought past the diversion. What to discuss?*

"Veronica, how's Claire?" I mentally slapped myself with that one.

"Little Claire so wanted to come and see you. But as it is a school night, she is staying with my mother and father."

"Who's Claire?" Delilah looked from me to Veronica and back again.

"She's my daughter and Kade's helping me raise her. He's such a good dad." Veronica smiled at me with her eyes shining. If she were a cat, she'd be purring. I glanced over at Delilah. Her eyes were shining, too, but I expected for a vastly different reason.

"You have a daughter?" Delilah's words were low and raspy as they cut right through me. My heart shattered at the sadness, loss, and yearning in her eyes.

"Dee." I started. The shrill ring of her phone interrupted me.

"I've got to take this." She stood up, dabbing at her eyes. "Don't forget you need more meds in one hour." She strode from the room and out the front door. The screen door slammed in the breeze. My head spun with the look on her face. The loss of our child still hurt her, and I had inadvertently rubbed it in her face. I was such a dense fool. Sadness for what could have been for us filled me. How did one ever get over the loss? Was it even possible?

# Delilah

"MELANIE," I BREATHED into the phone. I hurried to the barn across the drive. "You couldn't have had better timing. Did you get my message?" Images of Kade and Veronica laughing together at me danced through my mind.

Her laugh sounded in my ear. "Yes, but first you have to elaborate on how good my timing is."

"Fine." The barn door swung open with a squeak. The horses stuck their heads over the stall doors as I walked past them to the office at the end of the barn. I shut the door and sunk into a worn-out office chair.

"Are you in the barn?" Melanie asked.

"I had to go where Kade can't sneak up on me," I sighed. I spun around in the office chair.

"Isn't he on crutches?"

"Yeah, so?" I grabbed a piece of twine off a hook and looped it around my fingers.

"How much sneaking can he possibly be doing?" She had a fair point with that one. "Just tell me what is going on." She sounded like she was talking around a mouthful of pins.

"Are you working?"

"I have a mother of the bride dress I am finishing. I can listen to you talk. Out with it, girl."

"A woman showed up today, claiming that she came to take care of Kade." I bunched my hair on the top of my head before letting it all fall back down, sighing. "Evidently, they are, or were, involved." I blew out a breath and my hair fell down my back.

"Did Kade say they were involved?"

"No," I answered.

"Did he give her a kiss or hold her hand or give any indication that they are a couple?" Melanie mumbled into the phone.

"Not really."

"O.K., being the voice of reason. Number one, why do you care? And number two it doesn't sound like they are an item." Melanie was always the practical one.

"But there's a child involved." I bit my fingernails. A horse neighed and stomped its feet.

Melanie sucked in her breath and coughed. "Ouch, pins...I think that you need to talk to him before getting too upset."

*She was right. Why did I care what he did with other women?* "You're right. Anyway, did you talk to Pete about when the vet is coming out to his place?"

"Of course, I am right." She paused and I could hear a heavy object being moved around. "He's coming out next week. He said that should be enough time to float all of your horses' teeth if you could trailer them over to Pete's ranch as he doesn't have time to drive over to Lindsay's place and work on them there. It would be a hundred dollars per horse." I sucked in my breath at that, but they did need their teeth worked on. A couple of the older horses were dropping their feed as they ate and losing weight. Plus, their teeth hadn't been looked at for over a year.

"O.K., that will work. There isn't a nice place to do them at Lindsay's anyway. They are all out in the pasture. Would Pete pick them up for me? I don't have the money, but they desperately need to be done. Jasper, the black Quarter horse, is dropping grain as he is eating."

"I know, I wish I could chip in, but I had to buy materials for the costumes for the San Antonio Opera."

"I'll figure it out." We finished the conversation, quickly. After Melanie hung up, I spun around in my chair. The barn was quiet in the morning. All the horses were happily munching hay. I steeled myself to face both Kisment brothers: Kade with his lady friend and Kaleb for an advance on my paycheck. I was not sure which one I was more nervous about.

# Kade

MY BLADDER WOKE ME up in the middle of the night. I made my way down the hall. The crutches made soft scuffing noises on the floor. The room Delilah was staying in was dark with the door open. *That was weird. It's late enough she should have been sleeping.* Kaleb settled Veronica at the end of the house in my parents' room. The light was on in the kitchen and voices drifted down the hall toward me.

"So, Kaleb, I know we agreed at the end of his recovery but that's why I need an advance." Delilah's voice was soft. A clink of a spoon in a bowl sounded. *She needed money. That was news to me. What could she possibly need money for?* She was living here for free while she was taking care of me.

"It sounds like they need it. He is a busy person so if you got into his schedule you can't pass it up."

"Kaleb, thank you so much." She let out a little squeal. I hopped closer to the doorway and peered. She jumped up from her seat and hugged him. "I'll go call Melanie." She bounded up and started towards me. "Oh, hi, Kade. I didn't see you there." She patted my arm and bounced to Kate's room as I wobbled to lean against the wall.

"What was that about?" I made my way into the kitchen. Kaleb looked up from his laptop screen.

"Delilah needs some money." He shrugged and went back to the screen.

"For what?"

He stopped and stared at me. "She has been here for almost four weeks. Do you ever talk to her?"

"Can't you tell me?" I asked as I poured water into a glass.

"Not my business. Talk to the girl, bonehead." *Great, he was back to calling me my childhood nickname. Evidently, that was the end of the discussion.* He shut the laptop and left the kitchen. Talk to the girl, I wish it were that easy. My throat got tight every time I tried.

# Chapter 12 October 4th

## Delilah

Between the thoughts of Kade and Veronica, the veterinary appointment, and checking in on Kade, I didn't get much sleep through the night. I tiptoed across the hall. With my fingertips, the door creaked open. Kade sat on the edge of his bed with the cast propped up on the mattress. His head cupped his hands. The t-shirt clung to his back and sweat beads popped out on his forehead and neck.

"Hey Kade," I stuck my head in. "Rough night?"

"You know it was. My leg aches no matter where I put it." He ran his fingers through his shaggy blonde hair. It stuck out at all angles. He glanced up at me with a half-smile though the corner of his eyes pinched in pain.

"I'll call Dr. Glanders in a bit and see if we can get you something stronger." I walked across the room and drew the curtains. The sunbeam fell across the floor. High heels clicked down the hall and the door swung open. Veronica stood at the threshold, holding a tray of fresh fruit, orange juice, and waffles.

"I made breakfast!" She strode into the room. Her broom skirt swishing with every step. She hesitated when her eyes fell on Kade. Her painted pink lips opened and closed. "Wow..."

"I look awful. I know." He grumbled. His face paled when she set the tray of food on his bedside table.

Veronica's face fell and her lips quivered. *Seriously, she's going to cry if Kade doesn't eat her breakfast.* I rolled my eyes as I watched Kade look nauseated and Veronica trying not to cry.

"Alright, Kade, why don't we get you in the shower? It'll make you feel better." I grabbed his crutches. "Then, you can eat the wonderful breakfast that Veronica made you." Placing the crutches next to him, I helped him up. Veronica smiled at me, and I nodded to her in acknowledgment.

Together, Kade and I inched our way through his room to the bathroom. As we reached the hall, Veronica hurried out behind us.

"I can help him." She edged between us. Kade hopped forward another step.

I stepped back and raised my eyebrows at her. "Be my guest, but he needs help getting in and out of the shower without getting his cast wet."

Her face paled. "Um." Doubt clouded her eyes.

"I'd rather have Delilah help me," Kade mumbled. "She's a professional."

A sigh of relief crossed her lips. "I'll wait for you in the kitchen." She leaned in and kissed him on the cheek. Her heels clicked down the hall back to the kitchen.

I flipped on the bathroom light and turned on the shower. "There's nothing going on with you and her?"

"There's nothing going on." He glared at me from under his brows.

"Doesn't sound like it." I rolled my eyes at him. I helped him get the cover over the cast. My hand gripped the bathroom doorknob when his voice stopped me.

"Dee, we need to talk, soon." The words were so soft it was hard to hear them over the running of the water.

I glanced over my shoulders at him. "Yes, we do, but maybe later." I stepped out of the bathroom. Shutting the door behind me, I rested my head against the door. He was right, but I didn't want to have that conversation.

# Kade

BY THE TIME I GOT OUT of the shower and dressed, Delilah was gone. Veronica stood in the kitchen. She wrapped a little apron over her broom skirt. Her red hair was tied back with a bandana. Kaleb sat at the table, slicing through a frittata.

"This is really good," he said between mouthfuls. Veronica beamed. He drank a huge gulp of orange juice. "Good morning, Kade."

"Hi, Kaleb." I slid into the chair next to him. Veronica slid a slice of frittata on a plate in front of me. "Where's Delilah?" I cut into the egg mixture.

"She's over at Pete's." Kaleb scooped up the rest of his breakfast and plopped it into his mouth. My eyes bounced up and settled on him as surprise ran through my body.

"What?"

He nodded. "The veterinarian is there today, and her horses have an appointment."

"She has horses?" *What was going on?* Delilah had always loved horses, but she hadn't once mentioned them.

"Dude, you need to talk to her." He stuffed his cowboy hat on his head, stood up, and took his plate to the sink. "Thanks for breakfast." He smiled a slow grin at her, and she blushed a crimson.

# SECOND CHANCE WITH MY BULL RIDER

"No problem at all."

"Kade, Delilah called Dr. Glanders this morning. He has a new prescription for you at the pharmacy." He turned and walked out the door. His spurs ringing with each step.

I drank my orange juice and thought about all the questions I had for Delilah. A chair pulled out next to me. The scraping noise stirred me from my ruminations. Veronica placed her elbows on the table and rested her chin on her hands. Her eyes glinted at me. I sighed.

"You're a good cook."

"Thank you." She settled back in the chair, dropping her hands to her lap.

"Kaleb usually makes breakfast, because Delilah is a horrible cook." Feeling guilty about my words, I glanced up at her. She nodded and watched me.

"We should head to town today." I pushed the rest of my food around my plate. "And pick up my prescription. And if you drive, I can take you on a tour of Sunnydale."

"I'd like that." She stood. "Let me go freshen up." She walked out of the kitchen with a bounce in her step.

I sighed. Women. I didn't know what to do with either one. My appetite left me as I thought about the one person I'd rather be with on the trip to town.

# Chapter 13 October 4th

## Delilah

A drill sounded next to my ear as I held Jasper's head for Doc, the local veterinarian. Jasper's sleepy head rested heavily on my shoulder as my back ached and my head pounded in time with the drill.

"He has some bad points in there," Doc said. He looked at me, his headlamp blinding me.

"He's been dropping a lot of feed lately." My eyes scrunched closed and I shifted his heavy head.

"Almost done." He finished with the power tool, rinsed Jasper's mouth, and did one final check. The mouth speculum clicked close and he slipped it off Jasper's head so he could check Jasper's front teeth. "He's all good, now. He should be able to eat much better with those sharp points taken off." I nodded as I wiped my hands on my jeans. He proceeded to fill out his notes and handed me an invoice. It was higher than I expected, but Kaleb had advanced more than enough to cover it. I sighed as I handed him the cash. Horses were expensive.

"You have a nice group of horses." He folded the cash into his back pocket. "When you get the therapeutic riding stable up and running, let me know. I'd love to help you out."

# SECOND CHANCE WITH MY BULL RIDER 121

"Thanks, that means a lot. Horses are always trying to injure themselves." I shook his weathered hand.

"Don't I know it." He laughed. "My wife keeps rescuing more from the kill pens every weekend. We now have more horses than cows on the place." He grabbed his equipment and headed out to the vet truck.

I closed Jasper into a stall so he could wake up without hurting himself and rubbed his forehead. "Well, old boy, you'll be able to eat better." His head hung to his knees as he slept off his sedation.

Whistling, Pete strode into the barn, throwing some hay to the horses that were awake from their procedures. He paused to rub his horse, Gaston, on the nose and whisper in his ear. Melanie found herself a good one in that man. He was kind and gentle. A pang pushed through my heart. I wish I had that, but the one man that was able to hold my interest was unavailable. Oh, how I wished things were different. He was at the Kisment house with Veronica; while, I was out here, perpetually single.

"Hey Dee," Pete approached where I was rubbing Jasper's head. "Are you going back to the ranch tonight?" I nodded. "Great. Can you give him this?" He handed me a large white envelope that was thick and heavy. My eyebrow quirked at it. "It's an engagement party invite. Melanie has yours." Pete said.

"Sure, no problem," I said. I looped Jasper's lead rope around the hook on the door. "When are you able to take the horses back to Lindsay's?"

"I was planning on tomorrow if you want to help," he said.

I nodded and turned to the door.

"A bunch of us are heading to Cowboy's Bar this evening for the band. You and Kade are welcome to join us." Pete drug a hose over to fill a bucket of water for Jasper.

I raised my eyebrow at him. "We aren't a couple."

"I know... Tell Kaleb too if it makes you feel better." He whistled as the water splashed into the empty bucket.

# Kade

VERONICA CHITTERED on and on while I attempted to concentrate on the bulls bucking on the TV. I rubbed at the headache brewing at my temple. The overhead fan whooshed around, spreading the stagnant air of the closed-up house. Our trip to town was short and sweet. Sunnydale was small and didn't have much for entertainment. Veronica didn't want to go to the cattle sale barn and watch the sale today, or stop at Susie's Café, or go to the park to watch the baseball game in progress. We stopped at the pharmacy that also sold alcohol and tacos. Then, headed home which was how I ended up in the living room watching TV while she talked to fill the silence. I couldn't concentrate on what she was saying because my leg pounded from the pain, counting the seconds until the medications kicked in. Shifting in my seat, I leaned against the back of the couch.

Delilah flounced into the house, her hair swinging with each step as the screen door slammed behind her. Outside, the wind whipped against the house, causing it to groan and shudder.

"A storm is coming," she drawled. She moved through the living room to the hallway to Kate's room. "By the way," she stuck her head back into the living room, tossing me a large envelope. "People are going to Cowboy's tonight. You're invited...Did you take your medications?"

"Yes, mother." I rolled my eyes at her, catching the envelope with one hand. "What's this?"

"An invite for Pete and Melanie's engagement party." She smirked before disappearing into the other room.

"A night out will be fun." Veronica clapped her hands together. "When are we going to go?"

"Usually the band starts at seven or eight," I said, watching the fan blades circle.

Veronica squeaked.

I winced. The pounding in my head increased to a blinding pain. "I'm going to my room." I reached for my crutches and hopped toward my bedroom. The door to Katie's room was cracked. Delilah sat in the middle of the bed hunched over a laptop. Her fingers flew over the keys with rapid clicks. I tapped the bottom of the door with the end of my crutch, causing the door to swing in more.

"Are you going?" My voice cracked and I cleared my throat.

Her head snapped up. "I don't know. You're taking Veronica?"

"Um..."

"It's fine. I don't know if I'm going. I have some things to do in town, so I'll see when I get done and how I feel."

She went back to typing on her computer. I wanted to tell her how there was nothing between Veronica and me. The only girl I wanted to go out with was her. The words caught as a tangled ball of yarn in my throat: scratchy and immovable. My shoulders sagged and I turned back to head to my room across the hall.

"Dee, I would like you to come," I said softly before shutting the door behind me.

By the time Veronica drove Kaleb and me to the bar, it was crowded. The band set up on a stage above the sawdust-covered dance floor. Several people leaned up against the wooden bar that ran against the back wall. Pete waved at us from a booth in the back corner. He had his other arm slung around a cute brunette. Damien sat next to him, nursing a beer.

"I see some people I need to talk to." Kaleb patted me on the back before slipping into the crowd.

"Veronica, these are my friends, Pete and Damien." I nodded to each.

She extended a well-manicured to each man. The brunette slid over closer to Pete, extending her hand.

"I'm Melanie. Delilah said you are staying at the ranch." Melanie pulled Veronica into a conversation while she slid closer to Pete. Damien retrieved a chair, so I didn't have to slide into the booth, which would've been hard with my cast. My eyes searched the sea of faces. My heart dropped when I couldn't find the one person that I wanted to be here. Pete and Damien grinned at me when I turned back to the table.

"Are you looking for someone in particular?" Damien leaned his elbows on the table. His empty glass resting between them.

"Or are you just stretching your neck?" Pete quipped, before stretching his arms behind his head. I didn't know what to say to either one. Both grinned at me with that mischievous twinkle in their eyes. A pang hit my chest. I missed my two best friends. We had been friends since grade school when Damien's family moved to town. I propped my bad leg on the edge of the booth.

"Nah, I'm just looking for Damien's next date." I shot back.

Damien snorted and Pete waved down a waitress. He held up five fingers. "I don't date, man. You know that." Damien muttered, mock glaring at me.

"You're missing out on the best part of life." Pete drew Melanie to his side and kissed her full on the lips. She blushed a deep pink before wrapping her hands around his neck and kissing him back.

I was happy for Pete, and a little jealous. Veronica's eyes bore holes into me. I caught her gaze and the corner of my mouth tipped up. Lindsay carried a tray with five beers over my head to set it down on our table.

"I didn't know you worked here, too." I grabbed a beer and handed her a couple of dollars.

"Yep, gotta make ends meet." She pocketed the change and passed out the rest of the glasses. "I might take up boarding horses, though." She snapped her gum. "If all horses are as easy as Delilah's"

"Delilah's?" Confusion clouded my mind. I glanced at the rest of the group, but they didn't seem bothered by Lindsay's comment and had moved on to other conversations.

Lindsay shrugged. "Yep, those ten horses are loving life on my uncle's ranch. My old horse is enjoying their company."

"Ten?" I felt like a broken record.

She nodded and hurried away to another table. The band started playing country songs. Pete drew Melanie onto the floor where they two-stepped and spun around. I sipped my drink while Damien stared down into his glass, watching the bubbles rise to the surface. Veronica slid closer to me. I could tell she wanted to dance, but I was still in a cast and not very stable. Again, my eyes searched the room for the one person I couldn't find. The song changed to a slow, romantic beat. Couples swayed on the dance floor as the lights dimmed.

"Kade, what's going on with us?" Veronica whispered, shooting looks over at Damien, who was staring out at the crowd with a scowl on his face. I turned towards her. I drew in a big breath about to answer when she placed her finger on my lips. "Let me continue first, I thought we had some sparks or something. But I realized I was wrong. I wish there were something between us. But you look at Delilah like the world revolves around her." My mouth opened and closed like a fish. "Is there anything between us?"

I shook my head. "I love you like a sister, and I care for you and little Claire because of Ben." She stood up and wrapped me in a hug. I hugged her back.

"Then go talk to her." She whispered as tears glistened in her eyes.

*What was with everyone and telling me to talk to Delilah?* At that moment, Delilah walked into the room. Our eyes met over Veronica's shoulder. Delilah's gaze hardened. She squeezed her way up to the bar to talk to Lindsay.

"I'm going home. I miss Claire. You take care, Kade Kisment. And don't forget to visit us soon." Veronica wiped away a tear, kissed my cheek, and walked to the door.

My emotions rolled. She knew, and I think everyone knew, except for me and Delilah. I gathered my crutches and made my way to the bar. Delilah leaned against the bar, flirting with a cowboy from another ranch. I elbowed my way in between them, cutting off the cowboy with a stare.

"Dee, we need to talk," I leaned in to whisper in her ear.

"No." She glared at me before placing her drink on the bar.

"Yes." I grabbed at her hand to keep her attention on me.

"Give me a good reason to talk to you instead of him." She gestured to the lanky cowboy next to me. I glanced at him. He tipped his hat back on his head and smiled broadly at me.

"You drive me crazy... just come outside." I tugged on her hand, catching her gaze. She stood still at that moment, her eyes searching my face.

"Okay." She left a couple of bills on the counter. I smirked at the cowboy before I maneuvered both of us through the crowd as best as I could with the crutches, meaning I didn't smash anyone's toes or spill anyone's beer.

The night air was cool and brisk, the stars twinkled in the sky, and a full moon lit up the parking lot. A couple of smokers vacated a bench when I came out. I hobbled over to it, nodding to them. I sank onto the rough-hewn wood and leaned my head against the block building. Cars flew by on the highway not far away. A couple argued by their truck and another couple kissed under a large palm tree. She blocked out the light from the moon as she stared down at me.

"What do you want to talk about?" She crossed her arms over her chest. The plaid shirt gaped showing a white tank underneath. I dragged my eyes up to her large brown ones. The mascara and eyeliner made them larger than ever. I missed the way they seem to peer into my soul. I cleared my throat.

"Do you want to sit next to me?" I slid over on the bench and she perched on the edge. "Veronica and I aren't together." Her eyebrows went up, but she didn't say a word. I swallowed against the lump in my throat and continued. "Her husband, Ben, was my traveling partner on the circuit... A bull made creamed corn out of his body...and ... I made a promise to him... to take of care her and Claire." Tears threatened as I thought about that day, the horribleness of the accident, and how fast he died. The words lodged in my throat. Delilah reached for my hand and stroked it with one long finger. "She is like a sister to me." I managed to croak out.

She wrapped me in a hug as I fought to keep my emotions together. "So not a current or ex-girlfriend?"

I shook my head.

"That's good. She was irritating the snot out of me. Hovering but not doing anything to help," she said with fire flashing in her eyes.

"She probably never had to care for a sick person before. Ben was very smart with their money. Both of his girls are set for life."

"Why do you have to care for them, then?" She tucked a piece of hair behind her ear and folded her feet under her.

"Veronica isn't good with money. I take care of their finances and provide emotional support for both her and her daughter. It isn't easy to lose someone." I drew back to stare into her eyes. The swirling browns and golds pulled me in as time stood still.

"I know. I lost you," she whispered. She leaned into me. Her lavender perfume engulfed me. Her full, pink lips parted inches from mine. With my heart hammering in my chest, I closed the gap and pressed against her. It was soft and slow, just a connection. Our lips moved against one another, rekindling a passion that was burned a long time ago. She pulled back from me. My fingers ran down her scalp to tangle in her black hair.

"Why do you need money so bad?" I asked, I had to know why.

"What?" Her forehead wrinkled as confusion colored her eyes.

"I overheard you and Kaleb talking the other day." I brushed my fingers over her cheek. She closed her eyes and leaned into my touch. Swallowing, I attempted to get the right words out to ask her about the money and the horses. "I assumed he is paying you to be my nurse, but why did you need an advance?" Her eyes snapped open as she leaned away from me. The loss of her warmth left me shivering. *Wrong words, Kade.* I wanted to take them back the minute I said them.

"I made a rash decision and now have to deal with the consequences." She twirled a bit of hair around her finger, not looking me in the eye.

"But tell me why. I might be able to help you." I grasped at the hand to still it, silently begging her to tell me what was going on. She stared at me for a long time, so long that I wasn't sure she was going to answer. She turned in her seat and brushed her hair back.

"Melanie and I are starting a therapeutic riding stable." Her shoulders drooped. "We had everything ready until Mr. Giffery died. Then, we had to start over. He was putting up the money for us and the land." Her spine straightened and she looked me in the eye, challenging me.

"But why do you need the money so bad?" *I thought she had a great job in the hospital.*

"I quit my job." Her eyes got wide and frantic. "I can't go back. I have anxiety attacks just thinking about going back to work in the hospital. Then Kaleb said I could take care of you for the amount I need." She smiled at me slyly. "As long as you follow the doctor's orders."

I didn't know what to say. She always tended to downplay how bad things were. With the little she told me, she must be hard up for cash and all to start a therapeutic riding stable.

"For kids?" I set my arm around the back of the bench to bring her in closer to me.

"Yep." She scrolled through her phone and pulled up pictures of a little girl with pigtails on a little brown pony.

"She sure is cute," I said, an ache settled deep inside of me.

"They make everything worth it." She gazed at the photo with love and my heart constricted for her. I pulled her into my arms and held her. This woman was everything my heart needed. All I had to do was convince her of it. Music floated through the open doors of the bar. She sighed and leaned her head against me as the stars twinkled in the night sky.

# Chapter 14 October 10th

## Kade

The usual clanging of pots and pans was absent this morning when I woke up. I rubbed the sleep from my eyes and tried to go back to the dream I was having about Delilah. I glanced at the clock next to my bed. The red numbers read nine o'clock in the morning. A late start for being on the ranch, but the regular ranch noise was quiet. I wondered where Dee was. She always had the house up and running before sunrise. I swung my legs over the side of the bed and reached for my walking boot. It was painful to walk in but better than crutches or the wheelchair. The first few strides sent pain radiating up my leg until it calmed down to a persistent ache. My stomach rumbled as I moved around the room.

I made my way down the hall with an awkward step, clomp. Kaleb sat at the kitchen table with the farm report crackling over the radio. The coffee pot was half full and newspapers covered every inch of the table. I poured myself a cup and took a swig. My nose wrinkled in disgust when the thick, chunky liquid filled my mouth.

"Yuck, what did you put in this?" I spit it out and dumped the rest of the pot down the drain. I proceeded to fill the pot with fresh coffee grounds and water.

"I couldn't remember how much to put in the machine." He shrugged, sipped his coffee, and turned the page of the newspaper he was reading.

"Where's Delilah today?" I rummaged through the freezer and found some frozen toaster pastries and plunked them into the toaster oven.

"She needed the day off." He turned the paper again without even looking up at me.

"Why?" A feeling of dread settled in my stomach. Something was off and I missed her already. When the pastries popped up, I gently tossed them from hand to hand before covering them with the little icing packages.

"None of my business," he grunted and pointed his finger at me. "But you should probably figure it out." Kaleb grabbed his coffee and shoved his hat on his head.

"Where are you going?" I clomped to the kitchen table and pulled a chair out with a loud squeak.

"To the barn. Too many dumb questions in here this morning." The door slammed behind him as he went to the barn.

"I should figure it out," I muttered to Zip.

He cocked his head at me and whined. I broke off a corner of the pastry and tossed it to him. He caught it out of the air, swallowed it whole, and barked for some more. I hobbled to the pantry and poured out some of his dog food in a bowl for breakfast.

"What does it mean?" I ran my fingers through my hair and scratched the back of my neck for a second before a light bulb went on. "Oh no," I said.

My stomach hit the floor and the sick feeling washed over me that wasn't from eating too many pastries. If I felt this way, how must she have felt about today? Like a buffoon, I forgot all about it.

I fumbled for my phone and turned on the screen. It was October 10th.

"Who would know where she's at in the middle of the week?"

I needed to see her. I needed to hold her. Zip didn't answer, not that I'd expected him to. He was busy crunching on the hard kibble. It was the middle of the week and all of Delilah's friends were working. Where would she go?

The only place a heartbroken girl would go would be her mother's house. I dialed a number that I hadn't dialed in over eleven years.

It rang a couple of times before a scratchy, tired voice answered. "Sunny's Flowers and Gifts, how can I help you?"

"I would like to order flowers for delivery. What do you have?"

"The usual. Roses, carnations, some sunflowers, there are a few calla lilies leftover from a wedding."

"How about two dozen roses. Make it with as many colors as you have."

"Alright, hang on." He put me on hold. Soft jazz played through the receiver. I hope I was right as to where she was.

"Ok, young man." A scratchy frail voice answered. "What would you like the card to say?" I thought for a moment. Were there words to express my feelings of sorrow, regret, and inadequacy?

"How about?

'Yet in these thoughts myself almost despising.

Haply I think on thee, and then my state,

Like to the lark at break of day arising

From sullen earth, sings hymns at heaven's gate;

For they sweet love remembered such wealth brings

That then I scorn to change my state with kings.'"

"Shakespeare?" The voice wheezed.

"Yup, Sonnet 29." A faint smile touched my lips as I remember how she loved to read Shakespeare to me on our picnics in high school.

"You must be in the doghouse, son. Where would you like them sent?"

"Yes, Sir, I am big time. To Delilah Allen. She should be at the Allen house on Fourth Street?" The line was quiet for a while. I could hear a pencil scratching.

"It's about time, Kade Kisment, that you sent that poor girl some flowers." The voice wheezed, again.

"Yes, Sir, it is long overdue."

## Delilah

MOM WAS IN THE KITCHEN getting some lemonade and cookies together. It didn't matter how many years had gone by because the hurt was always there. Some days, it sat in the back corner of my mind like an unwanted plant that did not wither and die. Other days, it screamed at me. Those days were the hardest for me, especially when I was at the therapeutic riding stable. Tabitha was a few years younger than my child would have been. Today, he or she should have been celebrating a birthday with their friends from school. Kade and I would have gotten married and had a bunch more children. I rubbed my abdomen slowly, remembering the pain of that day. It was something I would never forget.

"Here, you go, dear." Mom set the tray of cookies next to me. She slid a lawn chair over and bit into a cookie. "This may make you feel better." She waved a round golden disc covered in sugar. "It usually does."

I forced my lips upwards as I took the sugar cookie from her. "Thanks, this is good." The sugary goodness of the cookie burst over my tongue. They were usually my favorite, but this year it was different, especially with seeing Kade every day. It brought back memories and feelings that I buried all those years ago. A tightness spread in my chest. I breathed through the pain, but a tear escaped and rolled down my cheek.

"Everything will be alright." Mom patted my knee, before donning some sunglasses and crossing her legs. "Kade will realize that he loves you, eventually. He's not fast on the uptake...all those concussions probably don't help, either." She laughed.

"My mood has nothing to do with Kade." I scoffed and choked on my cookie. She pounded me on the back.

"Sure, it doesn't." She rolled her eyes at me. "You have been moody and crabby since you started working there. And I know you aren't just doing it for the money."

My mouth gaped at her. How could she possibly think that? Her index finger gently pushed upward on my chin, closing my mouth.

"He's the only one that has ever driven you crazy. Not even that Greg guy that you dated for a couple of weeks. He was *boring*." She patted my knee again and leaned back in her chair. There was no arguing with her. She was almost always right, especially about Greg. I couldn't believe I dated him for as long as I did. Sure, he was a doctor, but he was bland and needy. Not my style. I grabbed another cookie when the doorbell ring.

"You going to get that?" She asked, propping her feet up on a stool.

I dragged myself up off the chair as the doorbell rang again and shuffled to the front door to see a colorful array of roses blocking the view of the delivery boy. I swung open the door.

"Are you Delilah Allen?" The teenage voice squeaked.

"Yes, I am."

"Sign here, ma'am." A receipt book materialized from the flowers. I signed my name with a flourish. He handed me the large bouquet and scurried away. I turned to the kitchen when I spotted the note. I ripped the envelop open and removed the card. Tears pricked at the corners of my eyes. My heart swelled in my chest as I read the familiar lines. *How did he remember that was my favorite?* In shock, I carried the flowers and the note out to the patio where Mom was relaxing in the sun.

"What have you got?" Mom tilted her sunglasses up to take in the bouquet.

"Kade sent me flowers." I breathed. I couldn't believe it.

"It looks like two dozen roses to be more accurate." She pulled off her shades and admired the different colors. "I take it he remembers too." She raised an eyebrow at me as I shrugged.

"We've never talked about it."

"It looks like you should." She went back to her book.

I inhaled the scent of the roses. It was sweet and fragrant. My heart swelled. This was the first time Kade had ever acknowledged the day to me. Did he think about it too?

It was about time to find out.

# Chapter 15 October 10th

## Kade

The quiet afternoon was broken by a car door slamming. Birds sitting in the trees squawked at the intrusion of their nap time. I ran a soft brush down my appaloosa's back. The white with black spots shimmered in the afternoon sun coming from the window. Footsteps made their way to the barn and the heavy barn door creaked open. Delilah's voice cursed softly at the rust rollers. I continued to brush my horse. When I turned around, she was leaning over the half door. Her eyes were wide and misty looking like she had been crying. An overwhelming urge to wrap her in my arms and kiss her tears away surged through me. Instead, I set the brush down and step, clomp closer to her. I leaned on the door, waiting for her to speak first. Time seemed to stand still.

Delilah cleared her throat and pushed her hair back. "Thank you for the roses. They are beautiful."

"You're welcome." I slid my hand over hers and gave it a gentle squeeze. Sparks flew from our hands to my heart until tears leaked from her eyes and landed on our hands. I reached into my back pocket and pulled out my lucky handkerchief. I dabbed the silk against her cheeks, catching the tears. I slid it back into my pocket as I leaned into her.

"Is that your grandfather's?" Her eyes steady on the piece of fabric.

"It's the one he gave me on my sixteenth birthday."

She smiled slightly and looked off into space.

"Do you ever think of that day?" She sniffed and shook her hair, breaking into my one thought of kissing her.

"Yes." Most days I thought of how our lives would be different, probably happier. Could I tell her that? Would she be ready to hear my confessions? More tears leaked from her eyes.

"I think of what that kid would have been like," I said. I brushed her hair behind her ears. "I think about what our lives would have been like."

She turned those big doe eyes to me. I got lost in their swirling depths, drawing me into their pools. Her breath fell soft on my cheeks as our foreheads touched. Before I knew it, her lips latched onto mine. Her soft hands cupped the side of my face bringing her closer. I wove my hand into her hair and drew her closer to me. Our lips danced together. They were demanding and sweet. Bitter but powerful. She drew back, panting. Leaning against the doorframe, I placed a hand on my pounding heart.

She gave me a watery smile before turning to leave the barn.

"Dee, wait. Where are you going?" I called. She can't leave, not after a kiss like that. My feelings for her expanded and pushed against the barriers I'd put around them. I tried to maneuver out the door, but it was awkward with the boot. Hay tangled around my bum leg slowing me down and sawdust crept under my sock. By the time I got to the barn aisle, she was gone. That kiss was like no kiss before it. She wouldn't get to walk away from us without a fight from me. I latched the stall door before heading up after her.

The house was dark when I'd entered it. The curtains were drawn over the windows to keep the bright afternoon sun outside.

"Dee, are you in here?" My voice echoed in the kitchen. The counters were clean. Dishes were stacked. I made my way to the living room. It was quiet in there. "Dee, come on. Let's talk?"

A soft weeping came down the hall. I approached Katie's room and pushed open the door. The amount of pink in the room made me cringe until I looked down at the bed. Delilah was curled up, facing the wall, and hugging a pillow to her chest. My heart broke into a million more pieces. How could I be so selfish? This day was hard for me, but it was a thousand times worse for her. I crept towards her and made my way onto the bed. I wrapped my arms around her and the pillow.

"It's alright, baby, I'm here for you now." My lips placed a kiss on the top of her head. She snuggled closer to me as I held her as tight as possible. The lavender of her shampoo washed over me, mixing with the smell of sawdust and hay from the barn. We laid like that until she stopped crying and drifted off to sleep, the tension leaving her body. She leaned into me, molding her body to mine. Contentment and something else I hadn't felt in years stirred inside me, surprising me with the strength of my feelings for her. Her breaths came out in even puffs. My eyes grew heavy as the house got even darker. I struggled to stay awake for her, to be her strong protector.

# Delilah

MY EYES WERE SCRATCHY from all the crying and my head pounded like I had been out all-night drinking. The bed felt smaller than normal and an arm wrapped around my stomach. My back pressed into the hard planes of a man's chest. I turned over to come nose to nose with Kade. His soft breath blew across my skin sending my heart skittering. I traced his features to commit them to memory. I wanted to kiss him. *Come on, Delilah, he hurt you.* But he was extremely sweet yesterday. My self-conscious was at war with herself. What to do? At that moment, his eyes fluttered open and he smiled at me.

"Morning, beautiful." He pulled me closer to him. He was about to kiss me. My heart stammered and hammered. Then, he closed his eyes, sighed, and went back to sleep.

That was a close one. I pushed the quilt off us. Isn't that the quilt that is in the living room? It is not from Katie's ode-to-pink room. I slipped from his arms and tiptoed to the kitchen.

"Thank goodness, coffee," I muttered as I poured it into a tall ceramic mug. A chuckle behind me made me jump. Luckily, I caught the cup before it hit the counter.

"Good catch." Kaleb looked up from his paper. "Delilah, you look awful."

"Thanks," I snorted and grabbed a strawberry pastry. "Did you cover us up with a blanket?"

"Sure did. I didn't want you to get cold with all of your clothes on." He flipped the page and continued to read through the Classifieds. "I take it Kade did good?"

"I can't believe he remembers." I bit into the strawberry pastry, even though it was dry and crumbly.

"I think he has been hiding it from all of us for an awfully long time. That." He gestured to the vase of roses. "was all his idea."

If what Kaleb said was true, Kade had been hurting as much as I did. Wow, what a thought to wrap my head around. Did he leave me because of his pain? It wasn't because he was freed from me and our relationship?

The pastry turned to sand in my mouth. I gulped the hot coffee to rid myself of the unpleasant taste. My eyes watered as my tongue burned and the roof of my mouth scalded. Kaleb watched me from across the table. His eyebrows rose.

"Surprising, isn't it? To think that Kade may actually not be thinking only about himself?" He topped off my coffee cup. "It took me a long while to wrap my head around that one." He grabbed his hat off the counter and tossed it on his head. "See you later, kid."

The screen door shut behind him before I could even get in a word. I sat there in my chair until my coffee got cold. Did this change the way I felt about him? Was it all because he was hurt too? Is it enough to overcome him leaving me? What if I tell him about my feelings and he leaves, again?

No, it was best to keep everything close to my chest. I may not need a man, but I wanted the one sleeping in the pink bedroom. But what if he breaks my heart again?

# Chapter 16 October 17th

## Kade

My leg itched in the walking boot, so I loosened a strap to wedge my finger under the foam to scratch. Nervously, I paced around the kitchen. Everything was ready if only Delilah would get here. She met Melanie for breakfast in town hours ago to discuss more plans for the therapeutic riding stable. I missed her already. I looked at my watch and paced around the kitchen table. Step, clomp, step, clomp in time with my rapid heartbeat.

Finally, her car rumbled down the drive and slowed to a stop in front of the barn. She climbed out of her little car, whistling a tune. Her long black hair was tied into a braid that swung when she walked. A smile played on her lips as she scrolled through her phone while she made her way up the stairs. Her jeans hugged the curves of her hips and led down to red cowboy boots. She reached for the screen door when I swung it open for her. Her face lit up when her eyes met mine, and my heart fluttered in my chest as I took her in. My arm went out to usher her into the kitchen, placing my hand on her lower back and guided her further in. She walked past me.

"What's all this?" She gestured to the plump saddlebags sitting in the middle of the table and Zip sitting on the floor below them. His stump wagged and his tongue rolled out of his mouth.

"I have a surprise for you." I hobbled over to the table, handing her a saddlebag. "You take this one and follow me." I held out my hand. She slipped her small hand into mine and weaved her fingers with mine. Electricity buzzed in my palm and my breath hitched at the contact. Then, she leaned over and kissed my cheek, shocking me to my core. My heart dropped to the floor as I stared into her eyes. *Could she forgive me and love me again? Or was she just flirting?*

"What's the surprise?" She broke the moment by playfully pushing me on the shoulder.

"Just follow me." I led her out the door and to the barn in the back. In the barn aisle, Apache stood saddled. A chestnut mare tied next to him, dozing in the shaft of sunlight. "I thought I could take you out for lunch. Cowboy style." I winked at her. She giggled and blushed.

"How would that work?" She walked up to the mare and rubbed her forehead, brushing her forelock out of the way.

"Well, first you get on this pretty horse just waiting for you." I limped over to the mare and untied her. "Then, you follow me." I handed her reins to Delilah. I wanted to help her into the saddle, but my ribs were still tender. Plus, I did not have the upper body strength to lift her. Delilah snatched the reins from my hands and talked to the horse softly. She placed her foot into the stirrup and swung up with ease. I smiled to myself. *That's my girl.* I led Apache outside. I tapped his knees and he laid down to let me mount. I climbed into the saddle. Clucking to my horse, he stood up with a lurch.

"That's cool." Delilah rode up next to me.

"Only took a couple of days to teach him." I reached down and rubbed his neck. "He's pretty smart."

"Lead the way, cowboy."

I swallowed the lump in my throat as I urged him forward. This was my one chance to show Delilah how much she meant to me. My hand shook on the reins, turning him down the lane.

## Delilah

THAT WAS A NEAT TRICK to get Apache to lay down. I didn't know when he found time to teach his horse that. He rode ahead of me. The warm sun reflecting off Apache's white coat. Kade's broad shoulders stretched the cotton t-shirt tight when he set his cowboy hat on his head.

My little mare was agile and responsive. I urged her to keep up with Kade. She tossed her copper mane before moving off my legs into a bouncy jog to cover the ground between us. I sidled her up next to him as the red dirt path widened out to go through a hayfield. Even though it was the end of October, the grass was long and brushed the horses' bellies. A red fox sprang up from the grass and bounded away, and birds called to each other. I turned to Kade.

"Did you see him? Wasn't he a beauty?"

A smile broke across his face as he nodded at my questions. "He sure was," he said.

He sidestepped Apache closer and reached for my hand. It felt safe to be enclosed within his fingers. Our horses stepped together down the lane. My heart was beating out of control at the nearness of him, the fresh air, and the scent of leather. The saddles creaked with each stride and our horses swished their tails at the flies buzzing around. We rode like this for a while until we reached a gate at the end of the field. Kade maneuvered Apache close to the gate and opened it.

"Go ahead. I'll close it."

He rested his bad foot on top of the gate to hold it still while I guided my horse around and into the next pasture. The appaloosa nimbly sidestepped the gate shut and Kade latched it with a chain.

"Come on. It is not much farther now." Kade said.

The wind blew gently from down the hills. It tousled my hair, and I closed my eyes to enjoy the feeling of it on my face.

"Why don't you let her run for a bit." He chuckled at my expression. "I obviously can't."

He motioned to his walking boot. I looked at him with questioning eyes. He nodded. I whooped. I leaned forward in the saddle and urged her forward. She rocked back onto her hindquarters. She burst forward; neck extended. We flew across the ground. We galloped two laps of the field. The wind stung my cheeks, whipping my hair back from my face. I clutched the reins in both hands as I urged her on. She went faster, stretching her body out. We made another lap before pulling up next to Kade. He grinned at me and I tried to straighten my hair that had come out of its braid. His eyes twinkled and his lips parted. I rode my horse up to him and placed a kiss on his lips. A surprised look covered his face.

"Thank you for letting me ride her. She's awesome," I said.

He chuckled. "Come on. We are almost there."

He led us over a couple of hills to a stand of trees that bordered a creek. We walked the horses down to the trees and dismounted. Kade loosened the cinches and replaced their bridles with halters that were tied onto the saddles. The horses chomped on the grass under the shade of the trees.

"Wow, this is so peaceful." I wandered down to the creek and kicked off my boots before wiggling my toes in the water.

Kade came up behind me and placed his hands on my shoulders, gently rubbing small circles with his thumbs. "Hmm, that feels nice." I leaned into his hands. Closing my eyes, I tilted my head back. Kade gently pressed his lips to mine. Butterflies flew around in my stomach as I basked in his attentions.

"I brought us some lunch." He said before stepping back.

His hand sent tingles down my arm as he led me to a blanket spread out on the ground. He had a couple of peanut butter and jelly sandwiches set out next to a couple of cans of cola. I helped him down as the walking boot was awkward. He pulled me down next to him, wrapped me in his arms, and kissed the side of my neck. Shivers raced down my spine when I leaned into him. I twisted around and my lips met his. Fireworks exploded around us. He pulled away from me. His eyes swept from the top of my head to my lips, where they lingered.

"I wanted to talk to you." He cleared his throat. He leaned away and ran a hand through his hair. "So, I brought you out here... This is my favorite spot on the whole ranch."

"Ok," I urged him.

"I was an idiot." He pulled at his hair with his hands and stared out into the slow-moving creek. "I should've been with you that day." He swallowed as tears filled my eyes. "I was so afraid." He grabbed his hat and twisted it in his hands. My stomach twisting in knots from watching him. I placed my hand over his forearm, feeling the muscles bunch and tremor with my touch. "I didn't want to lose you or the baby and... when I walked into the hospital room and saw you." He gripped my hands squeezing them tightly. "I couldn't make myself stay." His eyes swung to me and searched my face. "And be the man you needed at that moment." He sighed.

"The grief made it hard to be with you... around my family... or even in Sunnydale."

He drew me closer and tucked me under his arm. His heart pounding and a slight sheen of sweat broke out on his skin. "I think it was why I traveled the country bull riding." He continued. "I had to get away."

His eyes locked with mine and I could see the pain and sorrow swirling in their depths. His voice cracked as he said, "I should've been there for you instead." He leaned to the side and pulled out his wallet, handing me a faded picture of me in the green prom dress. "My heart has always belonged to you, even if I couldn't, wouldn't acknowledge it...It's the only piece of you I carry with me." Tears fell from my eyes. He wiped them with his thumb. "Delilah, I love you with all my heart. Will you forgive me?"

I didn't know what to say. I'd always loved him, even from afar so I nodded and pressed my lips to his. I don't know if I could forgive him, but at this moment my heart was screaming at me to take him back. I just had to try.

"Kade, I love you too."

He wrapped his arms around me. Holding me close to his chest, he kissed the top of my head.

"From now on, I want to always be there for you." He popped the top of a can of cola. "I don't want to lose you ever again."

It was a perfect afternoon, but I didn't know how long it would last. I pushed the sense of foreboding down and concentrated on enjoying the afternoon. There were so many things we needed to discuss, but first, he had to heal up.

# Chapter 17 October 23rd

## Delilah

Grunts sounded from Kade's room across the hall. I stopped and listened. They came in regular intervals. *What was he doing?* Shifting the laundry basket to my hip, I pushed open his door with the tip of my fingers. The door swung in, brushing lightly against the rug on the floor.

Kade stood in the middle of the room facing a large mirror on the wall with his feet shoulder-width apart. The boot on his injured foot was planted on the floor, making his hips uneven. His white T-shirt was discarded in a pile on the floor. He raised and lowered a pair of dumbbells, working his shoulder and back muscles. The muscles contracted with each grunt. Sweat ran down the ridges of his hard torso. My fingers itched to run along the muscle that he was building and to catch the beads of sweat.

He caught my stare in the mirror and gave me a wink. A blush spread up my neck and face and the temperature in the room increased a few degrees.

"Do you like what you see?" He raised the weights above his head, flexing the muscles of his upper back, shoulders, and arms.

"As a physical specimen, you're shaping up quite well." My grip on the basket loosened and it dropped to the floor.

He raised his eyebrows at me before moving to bicep curls. My mouth went dry and my tongue wooden. All the thoughts left me except how much my hormones like his body. I swallowed a couple of times and cleared my throat.

Kade was still watching me in the mirror and flashed me his debonair smile. It was THEE smile. The one that melted all my arguments with him and made my heart sing. I felt myself falling even more for him.

"When you're done working out, do you want to come to see my horses?" I gathered the bedsheets into the basket.

Kade's body stilled and he slowly turned around. His blue eyes sparkled as he smiled. "I'd love to." The words were soft and breathy. "It would mean a lot to me." He moved to come closer to me.

My hand extended halting his forward progress. "Finish lifting and take a shower." I wrinkled my nose. "You smell." Picking up my basket, I turned to the door and his laughter followed me out.

Forty-five minutes later, I sat at the kitchen table reading the comics from the paper when Kade's signature step, clomp, step, clomp echoed down the hall. Turning toward the noise, my breath caught. He wore pressed blue jeans and a button-down shirt. His black cowboy hat rested in his palm.

"I'm ready." The Texas twang thickened his voice.

"You look...great," I said numbly. He chuckled and step, clomp over to me. Leaning down, his lips brushed my temple.

The screen door slammed shut with a bang and a gust of wind rushed through the kitchen. It caught the newspaper and scattered it around the room. Kaleb strode in followed by a couple of his ranch hands. He passed the coffee pot around and each person filled their thermos.

"It's a blustery day today." Kaleb sipped at the coffee. The ranch hands nodded to me and Kade before leaving.

Slipping my jacket on, I stood up from the table and placed my coffee cup in the sink. "Kade and I are heading over to Lindsay's place."

Kaleb nodded, his dark blue eyes watching us closely.

"I'm going to introduce Kade to my horses." I shoved my hat on my head and pulled my ponytail through the space in the back.

Kade and Kaleb locked eyes. I looked from one brother to another, trying to decipher their unspoken conversation. Eventually, Kaleb broke the staring contest with a shake of his head.

"I'm not doing it," he growled. "I told you that before."

Kade's eyes flashed to me before settling back on his brother. Panic stirred in their depth for a moment. "Please." He stepped toward Kaleb.

"No." Kaleb slammed his coffee cup on the table. Coffee sloshed over the edges, staining the newspaper. "I'm not helping you kill yourself. Ask your other brother." He glowered at Kade and left the room.

"What was that about?" I cocked my head to the side and my forehead pulled into a frown.

"Nothing." His eyes skittered past mine. "Let's go see your horses." He held the door open for me to proceed him.

The ride to the Wilson ranch was quiet. Kade stared out the window and hummed along with the old country song playing on the radio. A nagging feeling bothered me the whole drive. There was something he was keeping from me. Something big. My mind searched for a way to bring it up, but I kept drawing a blank. I sighed in relief when the sign for the ranch appeared ahead. Steering the car up the drive, I itched to break the silence.

"Lindsay and her uncle have been wonderful to me," I said softly.

"That's nice." He said distractedly. "Are you paying board?"

"No, just chipping in for hay. Lindsay said they have plenty of pasture since they no longer have cows." I steered my car around a tree that had grown up in the middle of the driveway.

"Really? Since when?" He glanced around. The pastures were overgrown with old grass and weeds. Mesquite trees dotted the once open fields, and fences sagged or were pulled down with vines.

I shrugged. "I don't know. The last couple of years." I rubbed the ache forming between my eyes. "After his wife died, he couldn't do the ranching anymore, even with Lindsay's help." The barn came into view. The siding was stripped of all its paint and had weathered to a depressing gray. It leaned haphazardly to the side, only to be held up by a tree.

"It's a little rundown around here." Kade grabbed his hat and exited the door, shutting the door behind him.

Shaking my head, I followed him. At the fence, I whistled two short beats, and a pounding of hooves answered. Billy led the herd with Penny at his heels while Jasper brought up the rear. I climbed the fence, rubbed their foreheads, and feed them chunks of carrots. "This big black one is Billy. And Penny is the copper pony." I petted and whispered to each horse as I introduced them to Kade.

"That's a fine group you have." He leaned on the fence and ignored Penny's nose nudging him.

"I'm excited about the therapeutic riding stables." I proceeded to outline mine and Melanie's plans for him. He nodded along and absently petted Penny's nose. "What do you think?"

"It sounds like a plan." He rested his booted foot on the bottom rail. I settled against the fence and watched the horses mill around.

"So..." I cleared my throat and watched him from the corner of my eye. He stiffened. "What did you want Kaleb to do for you? Maybe I can do it for you?" I held my breath, waiting on him.

He picked a long piece of grass and chewed on it. "Um...don't worry about it."

"No, seriously."

He sighed. "Fine, I wanted Kaleb to set up my drop barrel." He muttered.

"Your drop barrel?"

"You know, the barrel suspended from the pulleys and springs in the barn." He picked his teeth with the piece of grass.

"Why do you need it?" I didn't understand it at all. I rubbed at my forehead, again.

"To practice my bull riding techniques." He gazed off out into the distance, ignoring my frown.

"Now, why would you need to do that?" I crossed my arms and glared at him. Anger building within.

"In case, I can ride at the Bull Riding Finals." He muttered.

I stared at him. I couldn't believe my ears. Was he planning on riding if he got released? I snorted. There was no way Dr. Glanders would approve of him riding. Dr. Glanders was a stickler for enough recovery time.

Kade cut his gaze to me, his expression was unreadable.

"You won't be ready." I laughed, bitterly.

He studied me for a bit and threw his piece of grass to the side. "Forget I mentioned it." He turned and step/clomp back to the car.

# Chapter 18 October 23rd

## Kade

The ride back to the Kisment ranch was quiet. Delilah tried to start conversations, but I ignored her. I knew that everyone, except for my brother Kurt, didn't understand. They didn't understand the drive to win, how I worked my whole bull riding career to be in this spot. I was first in the nation before my accident and had now fallen to fifth, but the gold buckle was still within my reach. I needed to go, to prove myself, to fulfill my dreams.

Sighing, I glanced at the woman next to me. My heart filled with love for her, but it had hurt when she laughed at my chances of riding. I thought she knew how much this meant for me, how I had dreamed about this chance. Did she think I couldn't do it? Did she not want me to ride anymore? Or was she just worried about my safety? I placed my forehead on the cool pane of the window and closed my eyes. How was I going to persuade her?

"I'm going for a ride," I said when we parked by the house. "Do you want to come with me?" I rested my hand on the door handle.

Delilah hit the lock button and turned to look at me. "We need to talk." She tucked a strand of hair behind her ear.

Those dreaded words that no man wants to hear. I closed my eyes and sighed. "Fine."

The seat creaked as she sild sideways and crossed her legs. She placed her hand over mine and squeezed. "Are you seriously considering riding at the finals?" She blew out a large breath and her eyes searched mine.

I turned my hand over and held hers between both of mine. My thumb ran over the creases in her palm. Lavender filled the car and filtered into my lungs. My eyes found hers. They sucked me into the depths. My love for her surged within me. I needed her in my life, but I also needed to ride in the finals. How do I explain how much she meant to me and how much bull riding means to me? I cleared my throat and reached out to tuck her loose strand behind her ear.

"Dee, you mean the world to me." I slid my hand under her hair and rested it on the nape of her neck. "I need to ride at the finals." She tried to pull away, and I leaned toward her until her back rested against the door. "I love you so much and hopefully you'll support me in this." She wrinkled her forehead. "If Dr. Glanders approves, of course."

She swallowed. "Why do you need to ride so badly? What if you have an accident and die?"

"I need to do this to prove to myself I can do it. This might be the only time that I can win the Bull Riding Finals."

She tilted her head to the side and squinted at me.

I cleared my throat and released her hands. I ran my fingers through my hair to stared out the side window. "I've failed so much in my life...I failed you when you needed me. I couldn't be the man you needed...I've worked so hard to get to the finals and...I need to ride to finish the season."

A tight smile pulled at the edges of her lips. She grabbed my hand, again. "Let's just see what Dr. Glanders says at your recheck." She climbed over the armrest and placed her forehead against mine. "I need you in my life and I can't go through losing you again." Her voice broke. "I love you too much. Please, stay in my life." She pressed her lips against mine. "Now, let's go riding."

# Chapter 19 November 9th

## Delilah

The drive into San Antonio was quiet. I drove and Kade stared out the passenger window. I tapped my fingers on the steering wheel and popped my gum. Every time, it popped Kade would flinch.

"Can you stop that?" He growled at me. He turned his blue eyes toward me. I raised an eyebrow at him.

"Stop what?" I snapped my gum again and he winced.

"The tapping and the thing you are doing with your gum."

"Oh, this." I blew a big bubble until it popped.

"Yes," he ground out.

"What is going on with you today? You're unusually cranky." I maneuvered the car through the parking garage. I wanted to find a closer spot to the hospital for him. Kade turned back to the window.

"Any spot will do," he said.

"Really? You want to walk all the way down from the eighth level?" I angled my car into a compact space by the elevator. Luckily, I drove a small car.

"I'm fine." He was opening the door before the car stopped. I sighed with frustration at him. The engine shut off and I grabbed his crutches before exiting the car. I hurried up to him and forced them into his hands.

"I'm fine." He step/clomp across the concrete

"Just use them. It hurts to see you limping and it's a long walk in your boot." He jerked himself away from me and entered the elevator. He pushed the button for the floor that we needed. Finally, I had him in a corner. I faced him and stared him down. I placed a hand on my hip and tossed my hair back.

"What is going on with you? You have been a bear to deal with all morning."

"Just nervous I guess," he said. He quirked an eyebrow at me.

My heart melted at his words. I slipped a hand into his and kissed his cheek. "I am here with you."

He squeezed my fingers back and his lips pulled up on one side.

"Besides, I am not scared of any doctors. I took great care of my patient." I raised my chin. Kade smiled and slid an arm behind me.

"Your patient couldn't have asked for a better nurse."

His lips hovered over mine for a brief second before closing the gap. The elevator pinged and the door slid open. He pressed a firm kiss to my lips, causing my knees to go weak. Then, he limped out the door, leaving behind the crutches. I sighed and grabbed them before the door closed again.

Kade held my hand in his as we slowly made our way to the orthopedic wing. He limped with every step as I carried the crutches under my arm, the carpet masked the thudding. After a few minutes, we made it to the waiting room. The glass windows let a large amount of sunlight into the room, warming plush chairs that were gathered in small groups around tables. A couple of TVs sat in the corners playing a daytime talk show. Kade checked in at the front desk as I made my way to a couple of chairs in a corner.

He hobbled over and sat on a chair and I drew up another to prop his injured leg up.

"They are running ahead of schedule. So, we shouldn't have to wait too long." He reached into his pocket and pulled out his phone.

"O.K." I flipped through a magazine as we waited. A few minutes passed before a nurse in bright pink scrubs appeared.

"Kade Kisment?" She called.

He nodded to her and I helped him up to his feet. He reached for my hand and squeezed it again. Butterflies danced in my stomach when I turned to him. He smiled back at me. We followed the nurse down a long hall until the last door. She motioned for us to go through.

"The radiology tech will be in for your x-rays. Then, the doctor will be in." She ushered us in and closed the door behind us. Kade hopped up on the examining table while I sat on the hard plastic chair. He rolled his sweatpants up to his knee. A knock sounded on the door and the tech motioned Kade to follow her to the radiology room. He winked at me as he followed her out.

Kade came back shortly and sat next to me. He gripped my hand and kissed the back of mine. Tingles ran up my arm and I leaned into his shoulder. Contentment flowed through me. My future life with him flashed before me. I smiled to myself.

"What are you smiling at?" He whispered in my ear. His breath sent shivers down my spine.

"Nothing...just thinking about us." I smiled at him, squeezing his hand.

A knock sounded on the door and Dr. Greg Glanders walked in, carrying a laptop under his arm.

"Good afternoon." He set the computer on the counter and made eye contact with each of us before pulling on some gloves. "How have you been doing?"

"Pretty good," Kade said. He took a couple of steps toward the exam table. A hitch was perceptible, but I could tell he was trying to hide it. The doctor glanced over at me when Kade sat on the table. I raised an eyebrow at him and shrugged. Dr. Glanders turned his attention back to the patient. He felt up and down Kade's leg and moved his ankle throughout its range of motion.

"Can you draw circles with your toes?" He watched while Kade rotated his foot in both directions. Dr. Glanders pulled up the x-rays. "Your fracture has healed. Everything is looking good on the radiographs." He drew out a pad of paper and started writing some instructions down. "Now you don't need to come back here, but you'll need two to three months of physical therapy to get full strength and mobility back. Here are the instructions for your therapist." He ripped off a sheet and handed it to Kade. "Any questions?"

"So, I am healed?" Kade unrolled his sweatpants.

"Yes, the bone is healed. But the ligaments still need some time to heal. Now, you must build up strength in the bone, muscle, and ligaments." Dr. Glanders said. He closed his laptop with a click.

"So, I am O.K. to ride again?" Kade said as he hopped down.

*What was he getting at?* I narrowed my eyes at him. *I am not sure I like where this is going. Didn't he hear Dr. Glanders that he needs two to three months of rehab?*

"Horses are fine, but no riding bulls." Dr. Glanders gave him a serious look. "It will take several weeks of physical therapy to even be strong enough to walk on it, much less run away from a bull." He walked out the door, closing it with a click.

"What?" Kade looked at me with a mischievous grin.

*What was he thinking?* I was so mad, steamrolled out of the top of my head and from my ears. I had to leave before I made a scene in the doctor's office. I turned on my heel and headed toward the parking garage. I arrived at my car before Kade did as he had to check out at the receptionist desk, and he could only hobble so fast. I paced back and forth by the car. My sneakers squished and squeaked on the pavement with every step I took. The temperature dropped while we were inside, and I shivered in my sweater. I crossed my arms over my chest and rubbed them as I continued to walk. The elevator doors dinged with arrival and slid open. Kade limped out.

"What was that all about?" He threw up his arms and gimped towards me.

"Are you seriously considering riding at the Bull Riding Finals?"

"Yes, this might be my last chance." He glared at me and I glared right back, wishing I could break all his bones, just to keep him home.

"That is ridiculous! Isn't it next week?" I threw my hands up in the air and shrieked. A couple of people hurried on by, diverting their gazes.

"Actually, in two days." He stood there watching me pace. That stopped me in my tracks. I walked up to him and stared him in the eye.

"Are you kidding? What kind of lunatic would put himself in that situation? You aren't in shape. You can barely walk, and you expect to be able to get on a bull and ride to win! In. Two. Days!" Worry gnawed at my belly and I felt sick.

"I only have to ride six bulls," he said softly.

My heart dropped and tears welled in my eyes. "Six?" I choked out. "But you're not in shape. What if you get bucked off and can't get out of the way? What if you dismount and land on your bad leg wrong? What if..." Kade placed his hands on my forearms and gently squeezed me. Tears fell and a sob broke loose.

"I'll be fine. Trust me," he said as he wiped a tear from my cheek.

"What if you don't come back? I can't lose you again."

He pulled me close to his chest and I soaked his shirt with my tears. "I have to try. This is the biggest event of my career."

"Why can't you just recover and plan to compete next year?" His hands rubbed up and down my back as my sobs quieted and I hiccupped.

"It's not that easy. I am ranked fifth in the nation. I have a shot at winning it. Next year, I start over at the bottom," he explained

"So, I don't understand. Don't you have enough money? Kaleb says you have it squirreled away somewhere," I said as I tried to pull away from him, but he held me tight.

"I'm one of the older guys riding. I'm running out of time," he said with panic in his voice.

"I don't want you to go. You need to stay here and recover. It's too dangerous," I pleaded with him as yet more tears wet my face.

"Baby, life's always dangerous." He placed a soft kiss on my forehead. "Let's go home."

He walked around to the passenger side and slid in. I wiped my tears on my sleeve and sat in the driver's side. I started the engine and turned my car toward the Kisment ranch. Tears continued to fall down my cheeks as the car fell silent and a pit formed in my stomach. This was bad. He wouldn't even consider not going.

About halfway home, I gasped and pulled the car over to the side of the road. New fears were threatening to surface. *Breathe in and breathe out, Delilah. You can do this.* On my third round of breathing, Kade interrupted me.

"Um, Dee, I don't mean to be dense. But what are you doing?" He reached out to touch my shoulder. I jerked away.

"Trying not to hyperventilate." I breathed in and out again.

"But why?"

"I may not make enough money!" I said. Desperation pawed at my chest and a large lump lodged in my throat. My chest tightened and I couldn't get air in and out. I placed my head against the cool glass.

"For?" Kade touched my arm again.

"For the therapeutic riding stable, you buffoon! I'm not able to get paid until you had a full recovery at six months or released from the doctor!"

He chuckled. "I wouldn't worry about that."

I shot him a look. *Not worry about it!? I was banking on that money.*

"You wouldn't understand," I said through clenched teeth. I tugged on the blinker to pull back out into traffic. "You never worry about anything." Silence met my remark. I finished the drive back to Sunnydale.

# Chapter 20 November 9th Later That Afternoon

## Kade

Zip laid on the plaid comforter with his head on his front feet. His eyes followed my every move as I walked back and forth across the room with my walking boot. My leg still ached with every step and turn, but the pain became part of my life.

"The doc said I shouldn't ride, and Dee doesn't want me to." I passed him on the bed. "But if I don't ride at the Bull Riding Finals, I'll lose my chance to win the championship." I ran my hands through my hair. "All those nights on the road, the rides, the eating fast food...everything here that I gave up with Delilah and my family. What do you think, Zip?"

He jumped up and gave a sharp bark.

"You're right." I tossed my old, black duffel bag on the bed. A couple of jeans, T-shirts, and button-up shirts landed next to the bag. I shoved everything in. I wrestled my good foot into the worn-out cowboy boot sitting next to the bed, shoving the other in the bag before zipping it up. "Dee is going to be mad, but maybe she'll come with me." A small sprout of hope unfurled in my chest.

Then, I slung my duffel bag over my shoulder and dug out my gear bag from the closet.

"Zip, time to go." He leaped off the bed and trotted to the door. His stumpy tail wagged in excitement. His nails clicked on the floor ahead of me when I opened the door to head down the hall.

Dee's singing floated from the kitchen when I approached. Her voice blended in harmony with the radio. She stood over the sink, peeling potatoes as a pot of stew simmered on the stove next to her. The aroma of beef and carrots caused my stomach to rumble. I'd forgotten to eat lunch today. Zip ran to the door and barked at the door handle.

"Oh, honey, do you need to go outside?" She asked in a sweet voice. She set the peeler and potatoes down. She turned toward the front door and froze when her eyes met mine. The blood drained from her face when her eyes roamed over my gear and bag. She leaned a hip against the counter and crossed her arms. "Really? Were you even going to say goodbye?" Her eyebrow raised as bitterness dripped from her tongue.

"Hey. Dee." I set my bags down and stepped towards her. She backed up against the counter and raised her hand, fending me off. "This is something I need to do." *How do I set into words how much this means to me?* "You have to understand. I don't want to have this fight again."

"You aren't ready." She crossed her arms and glared at me.

*I guess we were going to have it anyway.* "He said I could ride," I said. The corners of my lips pulled up into a small smile.

"No, he said you could ride a horse, but he wouldn't recommend bull riding." Her voice was hard when she turned back to the potatoes with her shoulders drooped slightly. "Don't let me stand in the way of your dreams, but then again, I've never been part of them."

The bite of her words stung and fractured my heart, causing pain as I struggled with my decision again. "I am sorry, Dee. But I must go. Please, come with me." I said softly.

She shook her head. "I can't watch you get hurt or die."

I wanted to take her in my arms, but everything in her body language said she didn't want to be touched and she didn't turn back around. I sighed before crossing the kitchen. The screen door screeched when I opened it, and Zip ran in front of me as we walked to my truck. He put his front two feet on the running boards for me to boost him into the passenger seat before sliding into the driver's seat. I turned my ancient truck down the driveway just as Kaleb rode up on his horse. He leaned down to peer into the truck window.

"Heading out?" He asked. The black horse he was riding stuck his nose in my hand.

"Yep," I said. I stared out the windshield trying not to think of how I hurt her, again.

"Delilah mad?" Kaleb lifted his hat from his head to wipe the sweat from his brow.

"Yep." My voice closed in around the words, and I tried to swallow the lump stuck in my throat.

"Thought she'd be. You still going?"

I nodded.

"In that case, drive safe and call Kurt," he said. He shrugged and shoved his cowboy hat back on his head.

"Thanks." I nodded at him.

Kaleb backed his horse away from the truck and rode over to the barn. I straightened the steering wheel to start on my way to the

Bull Riding Finals. I messed things up with Delilah, but I needed to do this. I could beg for forgiveness when I got back.

---

THE ROAD TO LAS VEGAS was a long trip, especially alone. Usually, I traveled out with some other riders from my area or met up on the way and we would caravan, but I'd been off the circuit for almost three months now and my usual driving partners were buddied up with other people.

"It's just you and me, Zip." I glanced at him. He had stretched out on the truck seat. His nose hung over the edge causing him to snort. He jerked at his name. "Well, and my thoughts." He huffed and went back to sleep.

There probably was a better way to handle the problem with Delilah but I needed to do this. If I was being perfectly honest with myself, I was getting too old to bull ride much longer. It was harder to stay in shape, I didn't have as much strength as I used to, and recovery was much longer than when I was younger. Next year, I may not even qualify to go to the Bull Riding Finals. It sucked getting old.

The highway stretched on for what seemed like forever and the markers ticked on by as the gas gauge slowly dropped until the needle came to rest on empty about an hour outside El Paso. I swung the truck around to park next to a beat-up gas pump. A strong wind rolled off the empty landscape, pulling at my hair and clothes when I climbed out of my truck. The area smelled of gasoline and motor oil. While I filled the tank with gas, Zip trotted to a nearby scrub bush to do his business. There was not much else around besides a little tan house adjacent to the gas station. The desert stretched out for miles in all directions. I squinted into the glare of the sun when a large bird circled overhead. The pump shut off and I headed into the small building to pay.

A bell chimed overhead as I entered. A young boy of eight sat on a high stool at the cash register.

"Mister, do you want a pop or candy?" His thin voice rasped.

"Nah, just the gasoline." I handed over my credit card. He punched a couple of buttons on the machine. He turned the card over and gasped.

"Mister, are you Kade Kisment, the bull rider?"

"I am." I smiled at his awestruck face. His eyes were as wide as saucers and his cheeks were rosy with excitement.

"Be right back." He dropped my card on the counter and sprinted through the back door to the little house. The screen door slammed shut and his high-pitched voice called to someone. Within a second or two, he came running back. A little girl was being dragged behind him, followed by a woman in a flower print dress. I pulled the cowboy hat from my head and held it in my hands.

"See Ma. It's really him."

I stretched out my hand to shake hers. "It's nice to meet you, ma'am."

"This is my ma and my little sister, Sara. We are huge fans of yours." The boy climbed back on to the stool to continue checking me out. The little girl clung to her ma's legs. I leaned over and winked at her. She blushed and hid her face in the dress.

"I apologize, Mr. Kisment. We watch bull riding on TV and you're his favorite." The woman blushed a little while watching her son finish the transaction. Love and pride shone through her eyes at the little boy. I imagined that's how Delilah would look at our child if there ever was one. It pulled at my heart that I may never have that family of my own if I didn't change something.

"Kade is fine," I said.

"Here's your card. Mr. Kade. Will you sign my poster?" He pulled out a large poster of a bull kicking up dust.

"Sure thing, kid." He handed me a marker. I signed the corner of the poster.

"Yippee! Thank you, Mr. Kade." He beamed at the poster. "I want to ride bulls just like you someday. Are you heading for the Bull Riding Finals?"

I nodded as I placed my cowboy hat on my head.

"Good luck, Mr. Kade."

"Thanks, kid. Y'all take care, now." I headed out to my truck. Zip looked at me through the back window, wagging his stumpy tail. I turned my truck towards Vegas as I watched the small family in my rear-view mirror. The woman had her hands on each child as they waved me away. I wished that were how Delilah had watched me go, but she probably never even left the kitchen counter. I drummed my fingers on the steering wheel as I thought about how I was going to fix this with her, after the Bull Riding Finals.

---

ANOTHER NINE HOURS went by before I finally arrived in Las Vegas. The city lit up the night sky like a beacon. Different colored lights flashed. People milled the walkways as I drove my beat-up truck to the hotel where the check-in was held and where all the riders were staying. A smart looking valet hurried to my driver's door when I pulled up. He handed me a card with a fancy number scrawled on it. I shoved the little card in my pocket and gave him a tip. Zip jumped out and sat next to me on the curb.

"I know it's tempting but don't take it for a test drive," I said, handing over the keys.

The valet laughed as he looked at the rust spots and worn-out seat. "I am holding out at least for a Corvette." He hopped in and drove away.

Another attendant stood waiting for my bags.

"It's fine. I got it." I swung my duffel bag over my one shoulder and hoisted the gear bag in the air. Zip lifted the corner of his lip at the man as we walked on by.

The sliding glass doors opened to the hotel lobby which was decorated in a chess theme. Everything was in black and white, except the employees wore red with black or white pawns on their backs. Alternating black and white tiles ran the length of the floor. In the corners, life-size knights on horses stood opposite of each other. A king and queen sat on thrones above the lobby on each side. Black plush chairs sat around a white table that faced a fireplace. On the table was a game of chess in action.

"How may I help you?" The clerk at the front desk asked.

"I am here for the Bull Riding Finals. My reservation should be under Kade Kisment." I set down my bags and leaned against the counter.

"Yes, I have you right here. You're in room 811. Take the elevator on the right and go to the eighth floor. The room shouldn't be too far down," he said. He slid the room keys across the white granite. "Check-in for riders is in the White Queen's Ballroom. Take the hallway to the left and go to the end."

"Thank you." I pocketed the keys as a whoop filled the air.

"Well, isn't it the unlucky Kade Kisment?" A voice called that made my shoulders tighten. I groaned inwardly, and Zip growled next to me. "Are you well enough to hang on for a couple of rides?"

"It's sure nice to see you too, Garcia." I turned towards the thin, tightly muscled Hispanic man. His large black cowboy hat sat low over his eyes. His western shirt was buttoned up and closed with a bolo and a large belt buckle graced his jeans. I extended my hand to him. He took it and weakly shook it. "I see you have been cleaning up without me in your way."

He chuckled before slapping me on the back "May the best or the luckiest cowboy win this weekend, Kisment."

"Yes, may skill beat out luck." I nodded to him and walked to the elevator. Zip was still growling at my heels. "It's fine, boy. He's obnoxious but harmless." The elevator door closed around us. "I don't like him either." I scratched behind his head as he licked my fingertips. "He has been the luckiest guy on the circuit, but I think his luck has just ran out."

# Chapter 21 November 9th

## Delilah

Frustration coursed through me as I ran my peeler around the potato, removing the last bit of skin from it. How could he? How could he just walk out that door like he is healthy as a horse? Did he not care about my feelings? What if he can't get out of the way and gets injured or killed by one of those bulls?

"Argh!" I groaned in frustration. I slung the skin into the sink, where it landed on top of my growing pile. I threw the clean potato into the other side of the sink well before grabbing the next one. A large rough hand caught my hand with the peeler. "Kade..." I said before I looked over my shoulder into the dark blue eyes of Kaleb.

"Take it easy on the potatoes," his voice was soft as he extracted the peeler from my fingers. "Everything will be alright."

"Did you see him? Did he really leave?" I had to ask the question. The ball of pain crept up my throat and my eyes filled with tears. I swallowed, fighting down the emotions.

Kaleb nodded to my questions. All the fears I had been holding in burst out as tears tracked down my cheeks. Looking startled and a little wild-eyed, Kaleb wrapped his arms around me and held me like a big brother would.

"He looked just as broken as you when I saw him," he said as he rubbed circles on my back.

"Is that supposed to make me feel better?" My voice muffled into the soft fabric of his shirt.

Kaleb chuckled and held me tighter, "I tried."

"What if he gets hurt again? What if he doesn't come home? He could die!" I said. I leaned away to search his face for an answer. The concern in his eyes radiated out towards me as I wiped at the tears on my cheeks.

"I hope he comes home. Kurt's flying out to watch him." He kissed the top of my head and headed down the hallway towards his bedroom. "And you don't have to cook supper." He called over his shoulder.

I went back to the potatoes. My knife chopped them into small even squares to get dropped into the stew. The rhythmic motions helped to give my hands a task to do as I stewed on Kade leaving. I pulled out my phone from my back pocket and rested it on the counter. Kade's smiling face from the ride we took a week ago flashed when I pressed the power button. The way the corner of his eyes crinkled when he smiled, and the memories of that ride pulled at my heart. Was I foolish to let him walk out the door? Should I have gone with him? He did ask me to go with him. A tear leaked out, rolled down my nose, and dripped to the counter. The phone buzzed and Melanie's name flashed against the screen. I scrambled to answer it before it went to voicemail.

"Hey girl, how are you? I saw Kade driving through town." She took a breath. "What's going on?"

"He left," I croaked out as the emotions of being left behind and everything the past couple of days welled up again. My hand shook so hard I had to set the knife down on the counter with a clatter. I ran the faucet to gulp some water to ease the knot in my throat.

"He left you?" Melanie's voice sounded incredulous.

"No, he went to Vegas to ride at the Bull Riding Finals." A sniffle escaped me.

"Honey, it's not the end of the world. He'll come home," she said.

"But we fought today. What if he doesn't? What if he hates me? What if he gets hurt? Or worse?" I voiced my worst fears to my best friend. A band of worry constricted around my chest as I gasped for air.

"Honey, calm down. I am sure he doesn't hate you. Pete's nanna once told Pete to let them go and if they come back it is meant to be. She is a wise woman."

"She is." I nodded in agreement.

"Why don't Pete and I come to get you? We can be there in a few minutes. Pack your things and you can stay with us for a while," she said. A car door slammed in the background and Pete's voice could be heard talking to Melanie.

"Okay." I set the lid on the stew pot. Anywhere was better than being here, where all the memories of Kade were.

---

A LITTLE WHILE LATER, Pete's truck rattled up the driveway and pulled up to a stop in front of the Kisment ranch house. The door slammed and Benny, Melanie's Beagle, ran around the yard, barking and terrorizing the squirrels and songbirds.

"Pete and Melanie are here," Kaleb called from the front porch. I'd just finished packing and grabbed my laptop and suitcase to head to the front of the house. Melanie hugged me hard when she saw me and Pete picked up my bag, carrying it to the truck.

"Come on. Let's go to Nanna's. She has your favorite peach cobbler ready for you."

Melanie led me to the truck and slid in next to Pete, so I rode shotgun. I rested my face on the cool glass while he drove the short distance to his ranch. Nanna was waiting on the porch when he put the truck in park.

"Come on dearie, I have just the cure for a broken heart," Nanna said.

Melanie handed me off to her. The old ranch house was warm and inviting like it was giving me a big hug. The smell of chocolatey goodness wafted out as Nanna led me into the kitchen. The worn oak table had seen its fair share of happy and sad events. The chairs groaned when we sat down, and Nanna ladled something out of a huge pot on the stove. I inhaled the chocolatey goodness when she set a steaming cup of hot chocolate in front of me.

"I added something special for you." She said with a twinkle in her eyes.

"Little marshmallows?" I asked hopefully. "I love the little marshmallows, especially the colorful ones."

She chuckled. "No, my special Bailey's. The only cure for a broken heart. That's what my mother made for me." She patted my arm and sat down across from me. "Now tell me what is going on."

Melanie dished out fresh peach cobbler for each of us and Pete excused himself to the barn. I gave Nanna a summary of what happened. More tears flowed from my eyes. Melanie scooped more peach cobbler, and Nanna made more hot chocolate.

"Now I don't know what to do," I dabbed at my eyes before scooping more peach cobbler in my mouth.

"You do nothing. You had that boy's best interests at heart. Men are like indoor cats. You can't tell them to do things. You've gotta let them do their own thing. They want to go outside, you let them." She sipped her hot chocolate. "If they come back inside, they are yours. You can't make them."

"But it hurts so much."

"Of course, it does. That's how you know your feelings for him are real." She topped off my cup with her Bailey's. "It will work out in the end. Just wait and see."

We finished our hot chocolate and peach cobbler in silence. Melanie sat across from me, twirling her engagement ring around her finger. Nanna picked up her latest knitting project. The needle points clacked away rhythmically. I swirled my cup of hot chocolate, watching the Bailey's mix with the hot chocolate. It was smooth and sweet. The chocolaty goodness made my heart feel better. The kitchen door burst open. Pete walked into the kitchen and leaned against the wood frame.

"I saddled up the horses. I think you and Melanie should go for a ride." He strode to the fridge and pulled out a can of cola.

"That sounds wonderful." My words slurred a bit as Melanie giggled. "How much did I have?" Nanna held up the bottle. It was halfway gone.

"Good thing I saddled my old horse for you." He held open the door to usher us out to the barn.

"Go on girls. The cool night air will sober you up." Nanna didn't look up from her knitting.

Pete tied his two horses up to the rail, Gaston, a big grey gelding, and Melanie's Belle stood next to him. She was a black as night Quarter horse mare. She suited Melanie perfectly. The first time Pete took Melanie for a ride, they beat him in a race. I walked up to the grey gelding and he pushed his soft nose into my hand, blowing out gently.

"Do you want to go for a ride?" I fished a peppermint from my pocket. He gently picked it up from my palm and crunched it. Pete helped Melanie up into Belle's saddle and then gave me a leg up onto Gaston's saddle. I settled myself on his broad back and brushed at his mane. My feet found the stirrups. I pushed my heels down and straightened my shoulders. "Hey, old man, take it easy with me."

I gripped the leather reins in my hand and nudged him after Melanie and Belle. We set off at a sedate walk with Gaston hanging his head low, his ears flicked around, catching all the sounds of the night. Melanie led us down a tractor path to a wide-open field. We walked to the center of the field and let our horses graze. The moon rose above and reflected a yellow light down on us. It was full and easy to see out in the darkness. Crickets chirped. An owl hooted in the distance. Coyotes howled and somewhere out in the distance, a wild pig grunted. The horses chewed contentedly on the grass. Melanie scooted Belle over next to Gaston so that she could talk to me without yelling. I leaned back in the saddle and rested my head on Gaston's rump. It was peaceful at night. The fracture of my heart softened just a bit.

"This is perfect," I mumbled. "I wonder where Kade is at tonight." Melanie's eyes flashed. She had been talking to him. "Have you heard from him?"

"Yeah, he said he was almost to El Paso when Pete talked to him."

"Hmmm, I hope he is doing ok." Silence met my statement. Time seemed to go by in slow motion as I watched a few wispy clouds float by the moon. "Was I in the wrong?" The clouds blocked a bit of the moon's shine before moving on.

Melanie cleared her throat. "You are not wrong to be worried about his health." That was all she was going to say, wasn't it?

"O.K." I shivered. "I think I'm ready to go back." I sat up in the saddle and grabbed the reins. Melanie led us back to the barn.

THE NEXT DAY, MELANIE and I sat on a couch in the living room of Nanna's house. She served us fresh brownies and ice cream as a treat after spending the morning riding horses. My laptop sat open to a browser page and Melanie typed furiously onto hers.

"I don't know if Kaleb is going to pay me." I broke the silence. My gum blew out in a large bubble before popping.

"Why do you say that?" She continued to type on her laptop.

"The agreement was if I stayed until Kade was better and released." I popped another bubble. "Kade was never released from care. The doctor recommended not riding but couldn't stop him if he wanted to go." I absentmindedly scrolled through my phone. Worry knotted on the bottom of my stomach as my heart slowly bled. I slumped into the pillows.

"Kade left. There was nothing you could've done to prevent that. You didn't quit." She looked up from her screen and smiled softly at me. "Kaleb doesn't seem the kind of guy to not pay you. Give it a little bit."

"If he doesn't pay me, I guess I'll have to go beg for my job back at the hospital." I wrinkled my nose at the thought.

"Do you want to go back?"

"Not really, I don't miss the stress or my co-workers." I sighed. "I'm ready for a change. It was nice to be out at the ranch and get into a routine. Maybe, Kaleb will hire me on as a cook or a stall hand?"

"It's going to take us forever to raise the money for the stables if you do that." She raised her perfectly shaped eyebrow at me. "Plus, if you do that, I'm not asking my parents for help. You'll be on your own."

"How cruel!" I clutched at my chest in mock horror. "You're killing me, Mel." She laughed and handed the last brownie to me.

"Will this make up for it?"

"A girl can never go wrong with chocolate."

Pete walked into the room and plopped onto the couch between Melanie and me. "Move over, girls." He stole the uneaten brownie from me and shoved it in his mouth. He reached for the remote to turn on the TV.

"Hey, that was my brownie!" I swatted him. He smiled a chocolaty toothed smile.

"I thought you would want to save room for Nanna's peach cobbler. It just came out of the oven."

"Seriously?"

He nodded.

I jumped up and ran to the kitchen where Nanna was holding a piping hot dish.

"I knew Pete would send you in here for this." She winked at me and placed a large heap of cobbler in a bowl with peach ice cream. "Here you go. Tell Melanie to come in if she wants some." She shooed me out of the kitchen.

Melanie and Pete snuggled together on one end of the couch when I returned. I had the other end to myself. I sat with my back against the armrest and propped my feet up on Pete's leg.

"What are we watching?" I asked. A sports announcer was on the screen running statistics.

"The Bull Riding Finals," Pete answered. "It is just round one." He balanced a notebook and pen on his other knee.

"What are you doing?" I gestured to the small notebook. Melanie rolled her eyes at me like I was foolish to ask.

"I am keeping track of what bloodlines of bulls do what, so I know who to breed my cows to in the spring."

"I forgot you had bucking bull cows." I settled into the cushions. "How many rounds are there?"

"There are six. Five regular rounds and one championship round. That's five days of bull riding." He rubbed his hands together like a child at a candy store.

"That's a lot," I muttered. I grabbed my phone and looked at the screen. I wanted to text him, and my fingers hovered over the glass.

"Don't you dare do it," Melanie demanded as she yanked the phone from my fingers. "He has hurt you enough. If he wants you back, make him grovel." Pete gave her a look that I didn't understand. "I know you disagree, Pete, but he needs to work for her." She pocketed my phone and crossed her arms.

We didn't say anything else as the bull riding had started. The bulls bucked and twisted, throwing guys off. Pete explained how the bulls and riders were judged and who was in each bull's pedigree.

"I never knew that stuff," I said after he was explaining about the different breeding programs around the country. The announcer said Kade Kisment was getting ready to go next. "Excuse me." I left the room. I couldn't bear to watch. People described traumatic events like watching a train wreck in slow motion. No thank you. I will go drink sweet tea with Nanna in the other room.

I walked in and she handed me a glass of sweet tea.

"I had a feeling you would be joining me soon." She rocked on her rocker as her knitting needles clicked away. Cheers went up in the living room a few seconds later. "I take it he stayed on." She winked at me as I got up to rejoin my friends. Relief swept through me. Only five more rounds to go. I sent a silent prayer that he would be safe.

# Chapter 22 November 14th

## Kade

I walked around Las Vegas in a daze. After riding Red Smoke in the final round a few hours earlier, nothing had felt real. The noise from the crowd was muted. The lights were dimmer. Taxis flew by me and people milled around. I had done it! I won the Bull Riding Finals Championship. Everything that I worked for the last eleven years paid off in beating Jose Garcia. The look on his face when I rode Red Smoke to 95 points was worth the drive out here. I walked back to the hotel and settled on a black bar stool facing a long white counter. The barman poured a whiskey neat the minute I walked in. It was my drink of choice for the last few nights I had been in Vegas.

"I hear congratulations are in order." He slung a towel over his shoulder and leaned against the bar. He pointed at the large screen in the corner where I was receiving the world championship buckle and talking to reporters. I nodded as I sipped the drink. "That's a big win. Drinks on the house tonight."

He slapped the counter before walking away. The amber liquid glittered in the fluorescent lights. It stung my throat as I took another pull of the drink. The stool next to me pulled out, and a busty blonde sidled on to it. She had been sitting in the corner with a couple of other girls. They were decked out in what city people call country outfits. Tight flannel shirts tied above their belly buttons, oddly shaped straw hats, enormous belt buckles paired with tiny Daisy Duke shorts that even Lindsay the waitress at Susie's Cafe wouldn't wear. The cowboy boots had pointed toes and not an ounce of manure on them. Dee would not be caught dead in that. She would be wearing her jeans and worn-out boots with a T-shirt. A ball cap with a horse would sit on top of her head. I shook my head to clear my thoughts

"What are you drinking, cowboy?" She batted her extra-long black eyelashes at me as her baby blue eyes latched on my left hand. She leaned her shoulder against mine. I tried not to cringe, so I slid my stool away from her.

"Whiskey." I emptied my drink and set it on the counter. The bartender filled my glass before walking away.

"What's a handsome guy like you sitting here by yourself?" She ran her hand up and down my bicep. Her fake red nails pinching the skin a bit. I slammed the next drink back.

"Thank you for the compliment. But I am in a relationship."

"But honey, she's not here. And I heard that you're a good time." She purred. She pressed her body into my shoulder. Definitely, a buckle bunny and only interested in one thing.

"I'm not interested." Her hand fell from my arm as I pulled away from her to head back to my room.

I shut the hotel door behind me and sat on my bed. It was lonely in the room. It was sterile with its white sheets and black floors and black and white furniture. I wished I had someone to share this moment with. Delilah was the one person I wished the most was here. My brother, Kurt, was fine, but he already flew home to Dallas. I wanted to see Delilah's smile and the way her eyes lit up when I looked at her. I wanted to feel her in my arms and to hear her voice first thing in the morning. I missed her more than I thought. I pulled out my phone. No text message or call from Delilah. Kaleb and the rest of my family sent their congratulations. Even my mother and father sent emails from wherever they were on their mission trip. Pete and Damien sent messages. But no message from the one person I wanted contact with more than anything. I sighed. My fingers punched in the numbers for her. It rang four times before going to voicemail. Her voice said to leave a message after the beep. I missed her to my core, and I wished every night she was here with me. I hoped I didn't ruin what we had forever. I prayed I didn't mess up so badly she wouldn't want me back. I hoped that she could understand why I had to do this. I hoped that she had watched me on TV. But all I could say was:

"Hey, Dee. It's me. Call me back."

# Chapter 23 December 20th

## Delilah

The wind was whipping through the streets, howling between the buildings. The rain slanted down and dribbled down my back. Shivers went up my spine as I ducked into the Post Office. The glass door slammed behind me. The wind buffeted against it. My hand shook as I inserted the key into my P.O. Box, inside was a form requesting a signature. I grabbed it and hurried over to the counter. Eddie, the postmaster, handed me a certified envelope after I signed the form. He gave me a toothless smile, before returning to sorting mail.

A sort of glee overcame the loneliness I had felt since Kade left. The return address was from Kaleb Kisment. The envelope tore open with a loud rip. My fingers fumbled with a piece of paper. I withdrew a check with a slip of notebook paper folded around it. On the paper, Kaleb wrote: *Thanks for everything that you have done. I gave you a bonus for getting him off the couch. Kaleb*

A smiled creased my face as I scanned the note for the second time. I glanced at the check. "Holy cow," My jaw dropped open at the amount written on the check. "That's a lot of money." My finger dialed Melanie's number on their own accord. She answered on the second ring.

"Hey Melanie, are you sitting down?"

"Should I be?"

"I got the money from Kaleb. You'll never guess how much is in there." I paused for dramatic effect. Lowering my voice and glancing around the Post Office. "There were sixty thousand dollars in the envelope."

She screamed on the other end. I slumped against the bench in the lobby. Sixty thousand dollars! I couldn't believe it.

"Did you count all the zeroes?" She breathed.

"Yes," I laughed. I scanned the check again. There were four zeroes. "I just double-checked and there are four."

Melanie screeched some more. The low tones of Pete's voice came through my earpiece. "Delilah got paid a load from Kisments!" I cringed as her voice hurt my eardrums. "I'm calling the bank in a minute once my excitement calms down."

My head spun with the money. It was what we needed. It would get our therapeutic riding stable off the ground. I leaped into the air and whooped. Eddie looked up from where he was sorting mail.

"Good news I take it?" He grinned. I nodded before racing to my car as the rain pelted down my back. Nothing was going to ruin my mood.

I pulled up outside of the bank. Melanie's little car slid into the parking spot next to me. I waved at her and then waved the check at her. She grinned back at me with a black folder tucked under her arm. We got out of our cars and dashed for the double glass doors of the bank. The warm air on the inside blasted us as I slid my arm into hers and we headed up to the counter. I signed the back of the check with a flourish before handing it over to the clerk.

"Can you put it in my business account?" I hopped up and down on my toes. She nodded as she typed rapidly on her keyboard. She handed over my receipt, said there would be a day or two hold until the funds transferred, and bid me a good day.

I turned to Melanie. "Now what?"

"We should talk to Mr. Dillard. I think he is in his office?" Melanie turned her gaze to his corner office.

Mr. Dillard leaned back in his chair, snacking on a bag of potato chips. His double chins wiggled as he chewed. Melanie looped my arm with hers and marched to his office. I struggled to keep up with her in her high heels and tight skirt. She knocked sharply on the door frame.

"Mr. Dillard, do you have a minute?" She turned on a megawatt smile towards him. He sputtered and wiped his fingers on the side of his shirt.

"Yes, ladies come in. What can I do for you?" He straightened in his seat and hastily stood up. He extended his beefy hand towards each of us. It was sweaty and sticky. I tried not to cringe with all the germs on it.

"Melanie and I have the money to secure the loan for our startup costs-" I started.

"Here's the business plan that we put together for the therapeutic riding stable." Melanie interrupted me and passed him the black folder. He paged through the several sheets that Melanie and I had pieced together.

"It looks good, ladies. We can get started on the paperwork. Have you found a place to rent or buy?" He settled back in his chair and stacked the papers on the side of the corner of his big desk.

"We are in the process of negotiating rental terms with Mr. Giffery's attorney." I shifted my weight from foot to foot. I met his gaze when his face fell.

"Sorry, girls. That property was bought this morning." My stomach dropped. The attorney was sure that he could work out a rental agreement until it was sold. It was a big piece of property that had been for sale for the last six months. "I can get the paperwork ready for the loan within the next couple of days. Think about where you want to have your new business. You can always check with a realtor." We would have to start over on our search, again. I drew in a deep breath and held it to hold the frustration at bay while Melanie had a blank look on her face.

We stood and left the bank.

"I could ask Pete if he could rent us some space for our therapeutic riding stable?" She twisted her hands. "I hate asking him though. The ranch is finally doing good on its own and he uses every available inch."

"It's alright. I may run the idea by Lindsay and her uncle, too." The rain had slacked when we got outside. The sun peaked through the clouds, glistening on the puddles in the parking lot. There had to be a place to rent. Tabitha and those other children needed a place to ride.

---

A COUPLE OF HOURS LATER, I bounced on my toes as I waited outside of Melanie's dress shop. She was due any moment to pick me up. The rain had finally stopped, and the sun was scorching the water off the sidewalk. I rolled my shoulders and pulled my baseball hat down to block the intense rays. Pete's truck came down Main Street. It sidled next to the curb. Its engine rumbling as Pete waved at me. I hurried over to the passenger side. Melanie slid across the worn seat. She wrapped her hand into Pete's.

"Pete said he found the perfect place to have the stable." She smiled over at me.

I jumped in the truck. "Really, where is it?"

"I'll show you." He pulled his sunglasses on and swung away from the curb.

I groaned. I forgot Pete loved to do surprises. The truck straightened out of town in the direction of the Kisment Ranch. My heart ached at the familiar sight. I reminded myself that maybe it wasn't meant to be. That's what Nanna had said. We'd been talking and texting, but I hadn't seen him in weeks, and last time we talked he wasn't coming home for a long time. Acres of hay fields and pasture ground rolled by. The driveway to the Kisment Ranch appeared next to us. Pete slowed the truck down but turned in the driveway across the road from the Kisment Ranch. Melanie's jaw dropped as I squealed.

"We were told it was sold," I said as I leaned out the windows.

"Yup, it was." He answered as he dodged potholes. The main house appeared on the left, but Pete followed the driveway to the right. Up ahead, a rambling white barn with a red roof opened into small paddocks. A large, covered arena sat next to the barn. When he pulled to a stop, Penny's head popped over her door. She nickered at us as we climbed out of the truck.

"How did you talk the new owners into renting to us?" I asked. I was in a daze. All the therapy horses were munching on hay in the stalls that lined the barn. Penny blew her nose in my direction as I searched my pockets for a peppermint.

"He didn't talk me into anything," Kade said softly behind me.

I spun around to find myself nose to nose with the most handsome man I had ever seen. His muscles rippled as he stepped forward and grasped my hands. He brought them to his lips and kissed my wrists. A tingle started in my hands and ran up my arms. I shivered slightly. His eyes shifted to my arms as he gently ran his hands up and down them.

"I've missed you these past couple of weeks. I've spent my whole life traveling, looking for that missing piece of me. But it was always you. You're the person that I think about every moment of every day." He pressed a soft kiss to my forehead. "It just took me a while to figure it out. Walking out that door for the second time in our relationship was the hardest thing I've ever done." He kissed the corners of my eyes and traveled to the tip of my nose. "I want you to be happy. So, with the money I won, I bought Mr. Giffery's place." He kissed me fully on the lips, slipping his hands around the back of my head, tilting it. My world was spinning, and I grasped on to his shoulders. He pulled back slightly. "I am donating the barn and the twenty-five acres here to your therapeutic riding stable."

I gasped and pulled him close for another kiss. Melanie and Pete cheered.

# Epilogue January

Delilah's heart was in her throat as the last few cowboys were getting ready to ride. It was the final round of the event. The cowboy that won this round went home with a shiny new Montana Silversmith buckle and a pile of money. The people on either side jostled her. She pulled her bulky coat close to her and stamped her feet. Chicago was cold in January and the wind whipped around the stadium.

The funnyman was on the arena floor, lighting sparklers and pulling pranks on his partner bullfighters. The crowd roared with laughter as one of the men's pants exploded, sending sparks into the air. The smell of sulfur and burnt cotton wafted to the stands. A concession man walked up and down the stairs hawking cotton candy and peanuts for sale. Delilah couldn't think about eating at this moment. Nerves fluttered in her belly and she twisted her hands in her lap. She sat on the edge of her seat as the announcer called Kade's name to be the final bull rider for the night.

"Please keep him safe." She murmured and clutched her seat

"Ladies and gentlemen, our last contestant for the night is our current champion, Kade Kisment!" The announcer called.

The crowd roared to life. Delilah leaped to her feet.

"He drew the big black bull named Hades, who has never been ridden. Can he do it?" *Queen* played over the speakers as the crowd stomped and clapped to the beat. Delilah strained to see Kade.

THIS PART ALWAYS PUMPED him up. The crowd cheering, clapping, and stomping. He slapped both thighs before throwing his leg over the chute. Hades was a big bull and filled up the chute from nose to tail. Kade settled his rope and crouched over his back. As he sat down, he slid his hand into the rope, tightening it down. Hades shook his horns and blew out snot.

"Alright, big fella. It's just you and me."

He ran a hand over Hades neck and shoulder. The bull stood still. Kade nodded. The chute swung open. Hades jumped two big jumps out, twisting his back to the side. He landed on the left lead and spun into a tight circle to the left. Kade kept over his hand, moving his free hand in time with the jumps. Hades reared straight up and kicked out before landing and spinning to the right. Kade moved his hips over to keep time with him. The sweat poured down his back and over his eyes. The buzzer rang out. Kade jumped free, landing on both feet. He tossed his hat into the crowd. A little girl caught it and beamed down at him. Delilah stood a little way down the fence. He climbed the gates and placed a big kiss on her lips.

"Folks, that was a 92-point ride! The winner is Kade Kisment!" The speakers crackled with his voice.

Kade was escorted to the top of the bull pit. A couple of girls in bikinis presented him with an oversized poster board check and a belt buckle and the announcer held the microphone in front of him.

"Congratulations, Kade. How does it feel to be the first person to ride Hades?"

"It felt great. He is a great bull who is cared for by a great stock contractor. I can't wait to ride him again."

"What can we expect in the up and coming months?"

"I'm working to stay at the top with good bulls and great rides." Kade paused and looked around the stage. He saw Delilah beaming at him from out in the stands. "None of this would've happened if it weren't for the dedication and love from my family…Delilah, sweetheart, I can't thank you enough for being my strength in the time of my greatest trial. Without you, I would be riding the couch eating potato chips and whining about my life." The crowd oohed and ahhed. Kade reached into his pocket and knelt on one knee. "I needed you in my life. It just took me a while to figure it out. I want what we have now to last forever. Will you marry me?"

Tears streamed down Delilah's face when the camera panned to her. She nodded her head vigorously. With a whoop, Kade vaulted from the stage and climbed the panels.

"I have loved you for as long as I can remember." He took her face in his hands and drew her in.

"I love you too." She murmured as his lips met hers. Fireworks erupted from the arena and the crowd cheered.

# Newsletter

Thank you for reading about Delilah and Kade! If you like what you are reading and want to keep in touch, sign up for my NEWSLETTER[1]. You will receive an Alternative Ending for joining the newsletter.

---

1. https://www.subscribepage.com/secondchancewithmybullrideraltend

# Don't miss out!

Visit the website below and you can sign up to receive emails whenever Allie Bock publishes a new book. There's no charge and no obligation.

https://books2read.com/r/B-A-HTMK-EZTIB

BOOKS 2 READ

Connecting independent readers to independent writers.

# Also by Allie Bock

**Cowboys of Sunnydale**
My Cowboy Crush
Falling For My Cowboy
Second Chance with My Bull Rider
My Unwanted Cowboy

Watch for more at www.alliebock.com.

# About the Author

After living all over the country, Allie resides in Minnesota where she spends the daylight hours working as a large animal veterinarian. In the evening, she escapes to imaginary worlds that reside within her mind. She loves to write about strong heroines that overcome adversary to fall in love with handsome cowboys.

When she is not working or writing, she can be found reading and spending time with the love of her life and their two Dachshunds. When they aren't in the house, they are working cows or riding their horses across open fields.

Read more at www.alliebock.com.